I0658680

The Bellmaker's Story

M. St. Croix

ISBN: 978-0-615-87249-0

for Veronica

"What if I told you the Afterlife is through this door. Only a few steps away. And the dead, who are very much alive, can now speak with us. No mumbo jumbo. No Ouija boards or scary ghosts. But clear, face to face contact with those who've passed on. Your loved ones, your Einsteins, Socrates, the Who's Who of all time. Brace yourselves, my friends. The curtain is rising on the Afterlife. Right here in this house. Come see for yourself. Come see the mystery of mysteries revealed. No longer will Death be our enemy. From now on it will be our confidant."

That's what the architect said. I remember every word. Pretty ironic, seeing where I am right now, since only days ago I stood there with the others huddled around him outside that door. 'Death's Door' he called it. He had names for everything. But I'm getting ahead of myself. You asked for a blow-by-blow account of the events that led to his disappearance. I can do that. And a lot more.

I'll start the day I arrived, staring through a bug-spattered windshield at cow pastures and cornfields with Otis Redding belting out his soul from my pickup's cassette player. I'd been six days on the road from San Francisco. Figured I'd reach the house mid-morning. Never happened. Not that my timing much mattered, I was two months late as it was. But after driving around lost in the Wisconsin boonies for more than an hour, I got antsy to find the place. So I doubled back to the nearest town of Newgrange. Stopped at a café to get better directions than the ones they'd faxed. But the cashier's directions were no help.

Miles later, I'm bumping up a rutted hill drumming out my frustration on the steering wheel when a car comes straight at me, airborne, like it's been launched, and for a split second frozen in space, its tires five feet off the road. Stomping on the brakes I swerved sharply to avoid a head-on. The car dropped with a whomp and skidded off into a shallow ditch in a blast of dust.

My body shook and burned. Before I could catch my breath, a dark van and a Jeep came hurtling over the hill in chase and screeched to a stop. Two men jumped from the van and ran to the ditched vehicle. A fleshy boulder in overalls extracted himself from the Jeep. I'd seen big men before but nothing like this rhinoceros. He charged over to my truck and rapped on the glass.

"Where you goin'?" he said, not moving his mouth.

I lowered the window. "What's all that about?"

"Where are you goin'?" he repeated, louder.

"The Sylvia House. Know how I get there without

getting killed?"

He leaned in to get a better look at me.

"You with the caterers?"

Ruddy face. A scalp of stubble. And there's a sharp, medicinal smell coming off him.

"No, I'm not a caterer." I reached over and grabbed the fax on the seat.

He looked over the fax squeezing a cue ball in his right hand until his knuckles turned white.

Someone shouted.

"Stay here," he said, stiff-lipped.

A word to the living. Never trust a man who speaks without moving his mouth. Telltale sign bad news is on the way.

The rhinoceros unclipped a walkie-talkie off his hip as he strutted over to look at the car in the ditch. From where I sat I couldn't see what they were doing or if the driver was hurt.

Waiting there, I recalled the cashier at the Newgrange café. A hairless, sad-eyed turtle of a man. I was halfway to my truck repeating the directions he'd just given me when the café screen door creaked and he called out, "You watch yourself now. Some folks never come out of that place."

Small town gossip, I thought at the time. *Idle minds whirring away on sugar donuts, caffeine and isolation.*

The rhino came back.

"So what's with the driver?" I asked.

He tossed the fax on my lap and pointed up the road.

"Left at the fork. Follow the fence line. Check in at

the gatehouse."

In the side mirror I saw a shirtless man being dragged from the ditch, shouting obscenities.

What the hell was he running away from?

Little did I know the very next day I'd be the one hauling ass over that hill trying to escape.

Taking the fork in the road I came to a tall, chain link fence topped with coils of razor wire. The keep-out vibe felt like a prison or military base. I followed the fence to an open iron gate with an empty guard shack. I pulled into a large lot where about thirty cars and trucks sat caked in dust. At the far end of the lot stood a lodge-looking building with a weathervane mounted on the roof.

Getting onto the grounds was like going through customs. After searching me, the twitchy little guy at the gatehouse dug through my backpack. He had me sign my name in a register, made a call to someone, then ushered me outside, pointing the way.

A cart path led me through a dense arbor. When I cleared the lilac trees and saw the house I laughed out loud. Rising before me stood a saltbox monstrosity three stories high. Sure it had the classic early American whitewashed siding, only the boards didn't run straight. Some ballooned out like a carnival mirror. The windows were all different sizes, warped and off-kilter. The shutters painted in Crayola colors. And smack in the middle of the façade was a squat little front door that looked tacked on as an afterthought.

A cartoon, I'm thinking, wondering if I took the

wrong path. *This can't be the work of Jean Tandre. Not the same architect who designed the Swiss Ether Temples.*

Around the grounds gardeners unrolled sod and planted saplings. Others strung up lights on bamboo poles. Golf carts came and went. One gardener stood in the labyrinth-like path ahead, his eyes locked on me, a walkie-talkie pressed to his lips.

That guy's no gardener. He's security dressed in overalls. Maybe everyone's in costume out here. Maybe Disney landed in a Wisconsin cornfield fourteen miles from the nearest town and built a funhouse for farm kids.

I came to the wooden bench where the gatehouse guy told me to wait. I set my backpack on the path and sat gawking at the house. No electrical wires anywhere. No antennas sticking out of the long, red and purple slate roof. Only a bright orange chimney propped at one end with a couple black hash marks that made it look like bricks. In a crooked third story window a looming silhouette glared down like a black crow perched on a high branch. I'm staring at the dark figure when a voice called out.

"You Gandy?"

A man in a white polo shirt came marching up, tapping a clipboard against his thigh. Pretty boy looks with sandy, surfer hair. Early 30's. My age, give or take a year.

"Yeah. You Julian?"

Julian was the head assistant of the place. He worked with both the architect, Jean Tandre, and the administrator, Leonard Roe. Roe's signature was on the advance check I'd received. Julian was the one who phoned to tell me I was hired, sight unseen. No bids or proposals. Simply an enticing description of the house they were building and Jean Tandre's desire for a harmonic bell.

"What are you doing here?" Julian sneered, looking me over like a mess he had to clean up.

"I'm late, I know." I stood and faced him.

"Late? You're ancient history. Didn't you get my messages? I must've called your studio like ten times."

I could've told him I'd been holed up and unreachable the past couple months after the tragic death of my girlfriend. But given his prickly attitude, I said I'd been on the road and left it at that.

He shook his head in disbelief. "Driving around for two months?"

"What's the problem?"

"You're the problem. Now hear this..." He thrust his right hand up to my ear and snapped his fingers. "You're not supposed to be here."

"Yeah, well are you seeing me? 'Cause here I am. And I'm not leaving until I check on the shipment of my bell. I also need to talk to Jean Tandre. Is he here?"

Must've said the magic words.

"Of all the fuckin' days." Julian shook his head. "Alright, come on, we'll have to get you set up."

I followed him along the curvy clay path to the front door, my legs still spongy from the drive.

"Jean Tandre," I asked again. "Is he around?"

I'd heard the stories about the eccentric French-American architect. Seen photos and drawings of his ether temples— giant, copper bullets sprouting out of the ground. I even brought along an interview where Tandre shared his principles of what he called 'vibrational architecture.' "Think of space as living energy," he told the reporter. "Consider the air itself as a field of conscious tissue that we chop and wall up into houses and buildings. How does it respond? Does it even have a say in the matter?"

"He's around," Julian muttered.

Good. I thought. *I can't wait to ask him what the "field of conscious tissue" thinks of this cockeyed construction.*

Julian opened the blue front door and everything changed. I was now entering a luxurious resort hotel with slabs of golden limestone covering the high walls. The floor and domed ceiling looked to be fashioned out of faceted blue glass or tesserae polished to a high sheen. Simply walking the floor felt like floating on a crystalline sea.

The lobby was bustling with people setting up easels and tables. Julian snaked his way around them. In the center a shimmering column of clear water, the diameter of a flagpole, fell silently from the apex of the domed ceiling straight through a hole in the floor without a splash.

Now this is the Jean Tandre I'd read about.

Still, the contrast of the outside and inside had me scratching my head for an explanation.

"This is Camie." Julian gestured to a striking, bronze-skinned young woman behind the reception counter. "She'll give you some documents to sign."

"About my bell," I said. "Do you know where it is?"

"Not a clue," he said, bearing into me with his pale

gray eyes. "Just be here in half an hour with your signed papers. Think you can do that?"

He clipped my shoulder as he walked away.

There was a time smug pricks like Julian would regret talking to me like an inferior. But I held back.

The guy's probably burned out trying to meet a killer deadline or satisfy some domineering boss.

Camie directed me kitty-corner across the lobby to a dining hall where a red-nosed man in a white chef coat spouted orders to people butting long dining tables end to end, forming a giant horseshoe. Carts rolled past with plates and silverware. Others hurried in from the kitchen with warming trays and coffee urns.

Caterers. So that's what the rhinoceros was talking about.

Camie sat me at the nearest table and handed me a stack of forms. "Everybody has to sign them," she said in a smoky voice with an accent I couldn't place.

The papers consisted of pages and pages of non-disclosure agreements and liability releases. "Read before you sign," my Grandpa always advised. Being a sculptor he knew all about contracts and their legal entanglements. "If you don't like the words, cross them out, or change them."

Although the legal jargon typical of these agreements had been replaced with common language, the gag rule stopped me cold:

> I hereby promise not to tell any person or persons about the premises, the architecture, the people, my experience, and the purpose of my visit from this day forward in perpetuity.

And then the kicker:

Even after I have died.

After I'm dead?

The strangeness of the place just got stranger. I re-read the clause to make sure it said what I thought it said.

It did.

Are lawyers now setting legal constraints on the soul? How the hell do they plan to enforce that? And why would the dead want to talk about this place-- even if they could speak?

No sooner did the thought enter my mind than a cloud of grief dropped over me like a tarp. Already I wanted to leave. It had been almost three months since Lucia's death yet her accident felt like it just happened. The mere mention of dying brought her loss caving in on me.

I pushed the papers away.

I'm not signing these. Since they don't want the bell there's no need for my signature on anything. I'll have it shipped back home and be gone.

Even if they wanted the harmonic bell, I wouldn't have signed their documents. Sure I needed the money, but I rejected promises of any kind, and these were absurdly demanding ones.

Lucia used to say it's an honor to be offered creative work no matter what the circumstances or who it's for. That you should embrace it like a cure, eagerly, gratefully, with open arms. But even Lucia might balk at this.

Talk about the place after I'm dead. Who are these people?

"Stop!" Someone shouted as a young girl burst out

the swinging doors to the kitchen on rollerblades, a sheep dog trotting at her heels. They rounded the dining tables, disrupting the chairs. Behind them, a blonde-haired woman appeared in the kitchen doorway commanding the girl stop. But it only egged her on.

Seeing me, the woman waved her hands in the air. "Little help there!"

I reached out to block the girl, but she ducked under my arm and raced out of the dining hall into the lobby giggling with sneaky delight.

"Please catch her before she breaks something!" the woman shouted.

What the hell.

I chased after the girl. She whirled around the people in the lobby. An accident waiting to happen. And sure enough a dolly, loaded with boxes, came wheeling around a corner. In a flash I snatched the girl's wrist and pulled her out of the way sparing her a concussion.

"Hey! Let go!" The girl's eyes flared in surprise.

"You need to watch where you're going."

"Let go of me right now!" She gritted her teeth and twisted her arm to break my grasp.

"You going to be careful?"

"No!"

"Then nothing doing."

The dog barked at me.

"Get him, Dingo!"

The girl's brick-colored hair flapped wildly across her face as she looked back to see if the woman was closing in.

She was already there.

"I owe you one, whoever you are," the woman said, taking the girl by the arm and tugging her away.

They didn't get very far before the girl broke free and sped back into the dining hall. Exasperated, the woman threw up her hands and stomped off after her.

"Did you sign the papers?" Camie asked, coming out from behind the reception counter.

"No, and I'm not. Do you know where I can find Jean Tandre?"

Before she could answer a throng of voices erupted from the corridor. I recognized the architect strutting among an entourage of people all talking at once.

"Jean Tandre." I lifted my hand.

The man, a bearded mountain, stopped in front of me, grand as a gorilla and decked out like some new age shaman in a crimson frock and a long vestment of gold embroidered feathers.

"Do I know you?" Tandre's eyebrows pinched together.

"I'm here with the bell."

"The bellmaker!" He grinned and pulled me into a tight bear hug. "Gandy, right?"

"Right. Joe Gandy."

"Ha!" Tandre turned to the others. "Everyone, this is Gandy, the bellmaker. I heard one of his bells in a New York shop called Sonic Showers. Out of this world."

His assistants politely quieted down and looked me over.

"I didn't think you'd make it," Tandre said. "Certainly, we must get you started." He gestured to the others, "I'll be right along."

Tandre led me down the corridor he had just come from and through the door of a design studio. He told me how he referred one of my bells to a landscape architect.

"She tried to reach you," he said. "Others have tried reaching you. Are you a recluse, or too busy to be bothered?"

The door flew open and the girl skated in.

"Jean!" the girl cried out.

"Mon ami! I was just coming to find you."

"Save me!"

"From who, my dear?"

"From school, who else!"

"Ah, school, that thief of time." Tandre hunkered down eye to eye with the girl. "I brought you something."

"You did?" The girl reached out to steady herself on Tandre's arm.

With the flourish of a magician, Tandre pulled a scarf from his coat and twirled it around the girl's neck in one fluid motion.

"A little something from an Argentine fabric designer I know. It's made from silk worms."

"Worms?" The girl made a face.

"Happy worms."

"C'est beau!" The girl's green eyes sparked while Tandre tied the purple scarf with a loose knot.

"And have you seen your Daddy today?"

"Yes. He's excited about tonight and…uh-oh. "

The girl's blonde pursuer stepped through the door.

"Ah-ha! I knew I'd find her with you! She's been impossible since she heard you were back, Jean. Come you little devil, reading time."

The woman forced a book into the girl's hand and towed her by the arm toward the door.

"See what Jean gave me!" The girl fingered her scarf.

"Yes, sweetie," the woman said, then gave a backward wave over her mop of blonde hair. "Welcome back, Jean!"

"Good to see you, Gudrun!" Tandre sang out then turned to me, "So, where's all your stuff?"

A voice crackled from a speaker on the wall, "Jean Tandre, you are needed in the lobby."

"You must forgive me. Party preparations. I'll be right back. Pour yourself some coffee. It's much better here than the dining hall. That stuff makes you scowl."

I wandered among the drafting tables. All neat and tidy. The floor swept clean. Framed illustrations and pencil sketches of fantastical structures covered the paneled walls. One captured my attention— a child's crayon drawing of a house.

This house.

All the crazy colors and odd windows. The whole façade identical.

So which came first, the exterior of the house or some kid's coloring?

Next to the drawing hung an enlarged photograph of a white-haired man in a wheelchair, his arm around a young girl. She looked like the roller-blade girl only a year or so younger.

Must be her grandfather, I thought as two men rushed into the studio.

"Excuse us," one said, nudging me back. "We need these for the celebration."

They lifted the drawing and photograph off the wall and carried them away.

A hardbound book of house plans lay open on a nearby table. Astounding plans. Three enormous domes fortified by vaulting trusses and mammoth beams. Domes that looked like the beaded, spherical ribbing of sea urchin shells.

What is this place?

The words of the cashier at the Newgrange café came back to me: "We seen'em come through town y'know, semi after semi thundering through here like an army convoy. But nobody tells us nothin' about what they're building out there. Like it's some big secret. It's creepy I tell'ya. Creepy like a cult."

Many features in the house plans had numbers beside them. I turned to the index pages and slid a finger down the rows of building components until I found Harmonic Bell - 1312. Then I flipped back to find the number 1312 at the front door.

"We're taking that too," a moving man said.

I backed up against a glass office door to give him room. The man closed the big book of plans and hefted it away.

A balsa wood model of the house sat on a massive desk inside the glassed office. The desk was made from a single slab of solid oak that stood on tree trunk legs, the bark attached. Medallions and certificates of distinguished merit from architectural organizations hung on the walls around the desk along with photographs of the construction site— Jean Tandre standing at a transit with surveyors. Tandre high up on scaffolding. Idle bulldozers buried in snow.

The two-foot high house model had movable, slotted sections that I started to dismantle when Tandre returned.

"You found it," he said, licking red sauce from his fingertips and smacking his lips. "So, tell me what you see?"

"Three large domes and two rectangular side wings that branch off to the north and south."

"The model only shows what's exposed above grade," Tandre said. "The domes are actually spherical."

"They extend under the ground?" I made a bowl-shape gesture with my hands.

"Completely."

I didn't ask the reason. Looking back at the model, I pointed to the dome situated behind the lobby.

"The Greenhouse," he said, relishing his design through my eyes.

"You growing your own food?"

"Not exactly."

"And this one?" I tapped the top of the third dome, beyond the Greenhouse.

"The Porch."

"A porch?"

"I wanted to call it the Bridge," Tandre explained. "But after living here in the Midwest, I realized the porch is the true coming-together place."

"So, where's the detail? There's just this empty hole in the model and nothing about it in the book of plans."

"Ah, that's a sacred secret." He tapped his temple.

"Drove the engineers mad. Just when they thought they had…"

Suddenly the office door swung open and in rushed Julian.

"There you are." He pointed a finger at me like an accused criminal. "I've been looking all over for you."

"Not now," Tandre said.

Julian lifted a sheaf of papers in the air. "He's not signed in."

"Catastrophe." Tandre raised the back of his hand to his forehead acting shocked.

Julian began to explain how things were now being done there, but Tandre would have none of it.

"Just leave them and leave."

Julian dangled a card key from his finger.

"What?" Tandre said.

"His room key, after he signs."

"No." Tandre shook his head. "He's not staying here. Gandy works with me. He'll stay up at the farmhouse. Have his luggage delivered there."

"I was told once we became operational all visitors were to stay in the main house."

"He's not a guest, he's an artist."

"But his project is not …"

Tandre cut him off again. "I said his work is with me."

"I'll have to bring it up with Roe."

Tandre's face hardened. He looked Julian in the eyes, his voice dropping an octave. "What happened to you Julian?"

"You were not there at the last meeting. Leonard

specifically…"

"Does Roe keep your balls in that basement vault of his?"

Julian's head ticked back. "New rules, man."

"Oh Julian, do you know what they're calling you?"

"Do you know what they call you?" he countered.

"Let's see, there's 'The Merry Monster,' and 'Jean Juan'. But my favorite is 'Johnnie God.' I'm sure there's more but no matter what name you call me, I'm still the one who composed the music and conducts this orchestra. Is that clear?" Tandre raised a finger. "So don't give me any of your petty Gestapo shit! You will have Gandy's things delivered to the farmhouse now!"

Julian's face whitened. He cocked his head at me. "Then have him sign these!"

He dropped the papers on Tandre's desk and flung the office door behind him with such force the glass would have shattered if the door had not been stopped mid-swing by the end of a silver-tipped cane.

"Leonard." Tandre's back straightened.

In the doorway stood a tall, lean figure. The crow I'd seen earlier in the crooked upper window.

So this is Roe, the administrator.

Just looking at the man felt like a spider crawling over my skin. Slick black hair. Ball peen eyes. And a finicky, pencil-line beard and moustache.

Roe gave an unspoken 'not now' joggle of his head to the exiting Julian, then fixed his eyes on Tandre.

"No word. No calls returned. Funny how silence is power."

"I said I'd be back for the grand opening," Tandre

said.

"And so the staff concocts a number of lurid and trashy scenarios. 'What if he's this? What if he's that?' Oh, Tandre will show up, I told them, unless he's in jail. And if he doesn't return, I'll put him there."

"I told you I had a personal issue to attend to."

"An issue or indulgence?" Roe said.

"What I choose to do with my time is outside your jurisdiction."

"Is it? And the lawsuits, the DUI's, the secret doctor bills, what? Do I need to unload it all here?" Roe pointed the apple-sized knob of his cane at Tandre's chest. "No! Until I have the final plans for the instrument there is no personal life outside or inside. Every breath, every blink of your eyes is mine. You want your freedom?" Roe held out his palm. "Stop stalling and hand over the final plans!"

"Congratulations, Leonard. It takes a lot of work to become a hollow man," Tandre slowed his cadence. "And yet I've watched you sweat to achieve just that. Shrinking master artisans into tiny black digits on white ledgers. Quite the collector you've become with so many little captives to covet. And so I ask myself, 'Is Leonard's soul that shallow?' Because from where I stand it looks as shallow and dark as a shadow on the dirt."

Roe drank it in, unflinching.

"You know the insurance company will not sign off without the plans. So, it's either something you're after or something you're afraid to give up. Knowing your history of destroying the things you create, I'd bet on the latter."

The tension sucked all the air out of the room. I recalled similar times on construction projects and art installations in their closing spasms— shattered nerves, relationships frayed. No different here. And every time I'd hear my Grandpa's voice in my ear, "Take no side. A tree gives fruit to all. Be a tree. What is your task?"

Wise advice. Too bad I never took him up on it.

"In here." Roe beckoned the moving men who stood frozen in the doorway. He pointed his cane at the house model. They lifted it off the desk with a groan, and shuffled it out.

Roe followed them to the door then pivoted from the waist. "I will not beg, Jean. I will not bargain. You may think you have plenty of playtime to tease and torment us before the millennium rings in. But the clock has stopped ticking. Your time is up."

The saying, 'character is fate' is only half true. It's really the interaction of characters that determines fate. And although the situation felt déjà vu to me, I had no idea how much hell was about to break loose.

After Roe left the office, Jean Tandre stood silent for a long moment. His bear of a body slightly hunched. His eyes fixed on nothing in particular.

"The workshop," I said, looking to snap him out of it. "The guy at the gatehouse said my bell crates might be there."

Tandre blinked out of his trance. "Ray would know. Let's get you to the barn."

He led me down the north corridor and out a side door where we climbed into a golf cart with the initials,

'J.T.' painted in gold on the hood.

"Forgive my outburst back there," Tandre said. "We've created a new wonder of the world and already people are staking claims."

"Julian told me over the phone the house was destined to become a landmark that would change the world forever."

"So that's what seduced you."

"That and the advance," I said.

Tandre grinned, then cooled. "I was eight years old when my mother died. For weeks after I could hear her voice right there in the room telling me what a good boy I was, to mind my Aunt and Uncle. Things like that."

He steered the cart onto a gravel road that curved up a hillside through a tall stand of pines.

"So I knew at a young age that the physical and spirit worlds overlapped. And it became a lifelong crusade of mine to connect the physical dimension to the other side, the Afterlife. Not merely to reveal it and see a spirit or two. No, to engage in an ongoing dialogue with the dead and share knowledge openly with the intent of bettering both worlds."

"What exactly did you build?"

"A trap. A vibrational trap. Not to imprison mind you, but to sustain a vibratory rate where transmission with the spirit world is possible any time."

"The Porch."

Tandre nodded. "A coming-together place."

"With the dead," I added.

"Nature has not been keeping the Afterlife from us.

Never has. At some traumatic point in our past we broke from the continuum and we've carried this separation from generation to generation for thousands of years thinking this is the way it is. Well it's not the way it has to be."

Tandre stopped the cart outside a big barn and shut off the engine.

"And until we tap more of our brain capacity to interact with these spiritual dimensions we have to create it through artifice."

From the outside it looked like the standard red American barn you'd see rendered in watercolor and hanging in a dentist's office. But this barn had been converted into a fully equipped production workshop with drill presses and table saws, welding gear, pneumatic hoists and pantograph cutters. At one time it must have really been cooking. Today it stood quiet. Like the studio— tables clear, workers gone.

"Anybody home?" Tandre hollered.

A pony-tailed man peered out from behind a motorcycle at the rear of the shop, a rag in his hand.

"Hey, Coyote." Tandre greeted him.

"JT," the man replied in a gruff voice. "Where the hell you been? Roe's been all over me."

Tandre walked toward the man opening his hefty arms for a hug.

The man shook him off. "Don't even think about it."

"This is Ray." Tandre tilted his head to me. "The man who helps our life run with only minor surgery."

"Hemorrhoids and hernias only."

Ray had a straggly beard and wore a tattered orange baseball cap. Stitched on the front were four words, YOU'RE LOOKING AT IT.

"Is it true you're staying on?" Tandre asked him.

"That's the plan."

"Will I see you at the party?"

"Wouldn't miss it for the world."

"Ray, meet Gandy, maker of bells."

"So, you finally decided to show up." Ray dropped the wipe-rag in the motorcycle's sidecar and threw a switch on the back wall. "These crates have been sitting out there for weeks."

The loading dock door lifted with a piercing squeal. Sunrays shone on Ray's pocked cheeks. Outside, an all terrain vehicle sat idle with two wooden crates on the trailer hitched to it. Ray pulled a pry bar off the wall and handed it to me.

"Ray knows where everything is," Tandre said. "You want something, go to Ray. You need someone to save your skin, ask Ray. And if you're looking to get some dirt on anybody, Ray's the hall of records."

"That's my survival insurance." He bit the filter off a cigarette and lit up.

Wedging the bar, I pried the lid off a crate. Then I freed the sides, removed the packing straw, and revealed the big bell. Ray glared at it owl-eyed. Somebody once described one of my bells as a tuba that swallowed a pagoda. Not the typical upside-down teacup shape you find hanging from church belfries.

"Your door bell," I said to Tandre.

By the man's bewildered expression I could tell he

was surprised by its size.

"That's…"

"Bigger than the one you saw in New York? Times four."

Tandre fingered his beard.

I tumped the bowl of the bell with my knuckles. "Want to hear it?"

Ray fetched the forklift and lifted the two hundred ninety-six pound harmonic bell off the trailer and drove it into the barn. Once inside I had Ray elevate it chest-high.

"Listen up." I raised the mallet. "In the beginning was the vibe."

Shifting the weight to my right leg, I coiled like a discus thrower, whipped the teak mallet around and struck the bowl of the bell.

BWOHHH-WOO-WAH-ONGGG!

Ray and Tandre's mouths puffed open as the bell rippled the air of the barn. Most first timers merely hear a big bong. But I could tell by their eyes and facial movements they were picking up the subtler changes. How the initial boom spawned a second tone that generated a third, each ascending in pitch. A shimmying metallic clatter gyrated from the machinery and tool lockers as resonant overtones sung free and clear. And lastly, the hum tone pushed out its deep, earthy thrum until it softly simmered away into space.

"Holy shit." Ray hopped down off the forklift. "Gimme fuckin' goose bumps."

"This is it!" Tandre said. "This is the ornament of the Sylvia House." He reached out his open palm toward me. "May I?"

"It's your bell."

I didn't mention the much smaller bell I'd shipped along just in case.

"It's perfect," he said as I handed him the mallet. "Perfect as a pinecone."

He shouldered the nine-pound mallet and then froze. "Ha! It's still ringing. Do you hear it?"

"I can feel it in my bones," Ray said.

"How long will it last?"

"One was clocked at ninety seconds," I said, pointing to the sweet spot on the bell for Tandre to aim the mallet.

"Ninety seconds."

"One strike."

"Well, time this."

Tandre stepped up to the bell. I noticed Ray punch a button on his wristwatch just before Tandre delivered the blow.

BWOHHH-WOO-WAH-ONGGG!

The three of us stood motionless, drenched in the booming well of sound. The sonic waves rolled through my body like ocean swells and all the tension I'd been carrying over the past few days lifted away.

"Who needs drugs," Ray said.

Tandre lifted a finger, nodding and nodding while the bell tone rung in the air seemingly forever before it finally faded out of earshot.

Ray clicked his watch.

"Fifty seconds, there abouts."

Tandre looked at me, wide-eyed. "Like getting a

massage, only on the inside."

"Ah, let's hang this sucker!" Ray shouted. "I know just the place— around Roe's neck."

Tandre choked up on the handle and tapped the mallet head into his palm.

"The plan was to suspend it at the front door of the house like a Sanctus bell to call people to gather."

"Was?"

"I'm thinking."

"No-no, your thinking days are over," Ray said.

Tandre lowered the mallet. He traced the tips of his fingers down the side of the bell where the sound bow met the reinforced rim.

"In medieval times bells were baptized by the church," Tandre said. "People would hang them outside their doors to repel evil spirits."

"The front door's a good place," I said. "Can't say it will repel evil spirits, but it will relax people before they enter."

"They're gonna need it," Ray said. "Only on their way out."

Tandre stooped to examine the interior of the bell.

"Lucia," he read the name etched inside the rim. "Is that the name of the foundry?"

"No." I shook my head.

Tandre ducked back out from under the bell. "Your muse?"

"My muse, my love, my …"

"These outer do-dads…" Ray interrupted, pointing to the flarings around the crown.

"To amplify," I explained. "I also tune the bell so

that it's in resonance with the spirit of the place."

"How's that?"

"I listen. And I use these."

I unrolled a leather sheath on the worktable. Inside it were eight calibrated tuning forks.

"I grind a bit off the bell's sound bow inside the rim where it's the thickest to deepen the pitch. And see the fins in here?" I tapped my finger inside the bell's crown.

Ray stuck his head inside the bell to see what I was pointing at.

"I can carefully shave them back until a harmonic resonance is achieved between the bell and the prime tone of the land."

"Prime tone? I'm not following, but hey, that's cool," Ray's voice echoed inside the bell.

"It's nuancey stuff. You'll know when you hear it."

"I love it," Tandre raised the mallet, "One more time?"

"Hit it," said Ray.

As Tandre locked his legs to strike the bell again, another bell sounded. It rang in sets of three repeated pings. Ray yanked a satellite phone from a pocket in his tool belt and stuck it to his ear.

"Yo. Who? Hang on." Ray handed the phone to Tandre, silently mouthing, "A woman."

Tandre whispered, "Who?"

Ray dropped the phone to his side. "I don't know who she is or how she got this number. We'll talk about that later. Right now she sounds pretty rattled."

Ray thrust the phone at Tandre. He took it and handed me the mallet.

"This is Jean," he said, strolling away, the bulky unit propped to his ear.

Ray watched Tandre leave the barn.

"God help us if it's another paternity thing." Ray took a deep drag on his cigarette and let out a growl of smoke. "Okay man," he extended an arm. "The shop is yours. The only ground rules: return all tools sharp and clean and sweep up after yourself. If you don't, I'll kill you with my bare hands. The first aid box is over there on the stair wall and the shitter's in the corner."

"Do you know where my luggage is?"

"What's it look like?"

"Big black duffel bag," I said.

Ray tamped out his cigarette on the fender of the forklift. "I'll check on it. First I got to fetch my phone or I'll never see it again."

He started to walk away.

"What's that?" I muttered, pointing at the open barn door.

"What?"

"That blue light that just flickered outside."

"Describe it."

I tried to explain what looked like a huge blue feather hovering in midair outside the barn. No head. No legs. Just one big luminous feather bright as a flame. It hung there for a couple seconds then vanished.

"So, you saw one. Not everyone does, including me." Ray stared outside the barn door. "They been appearing more and more lately, roaming the grounds. First time anyone's seen one up here on the hill. Must have heard your bell and come to check it out."

The feather-like vision came and went so fast I couldn't tell if it was a hallucination or a trick of the light. Never been one to scare easily, but the phantom-like thing gave my nerves a jolt.

After Ray left, I stood for a minute in the quiet of idle tools. I'd often dreamt of having a complete workshop like that and the yard of materials to go with it. The barn had rows of high windows along both sides with tinted glass that gave the light a rich, golden patina making you feel like you were working in a mystical place and time.

On a large worktable I emptied my backpack. Then ventured out behind the barn to the trailer and pulled my tools and supplies out of the second crate. At the corner of the barn stood a big, rusty iron farrier's vise, the kind a blacksmith would use to hammer out horseshoes a century ago. As I carried my things back to the barn, I saw Ray speaking to Tandre beside a shoulder-high stack of lumber.

"You know I never trusted any of them, including you," I overheard Ray say. "But it's gotten downright tyrannical. Right after you left things started getting insanely militant. Like a line's been drawn and ..."

Ray spotted me out the corner of his eye. He stopped talking and shot me a stay-away stare.

Back inside the barn I realized how hungry I'd become. I hadn't eaten all day and the food I'd brought along was in my duffel bag, wherever that was. The guy at the gatehouse took it from me.

When Ray returned he jammed the satellite phone

into his nail belt and walked up to the bell hanging from the forklift.

"JT hired you, right?"

"That's right," I said.

"And this thing here is all your own design, right?"

"Yeah, that thing there. Why?"

"Nothin'." He glanced at my hands, then at my eyes. "You just don't look like a bellmaker."

"And what do bellmakers look like?"

"Not like you. But I gotta say, that's some bell you made." He flicked the lip of the bell with a fingernail. "Is it bronze?"

"Not entirely. I added a mix of alloys that help the metal carry the tone at full throb longer and stronger."

"What alloys?"

"Sacred secret." I tapped my temple, echoing Tandre's words.

Ray wagged a finger at my face. "Don't. Don't you say that."

I changed the subject. "So, what was that thing I saw outside?"

"What thing?"

"The bright blue light I saw flash by."

"We'll get to that. Come on. JT asked me to set you up at the farmhouse."

I walked up the road beside Ray on his motorcycle. He told me how he'd been hired with three others to convert the barn into a working factory of sorts four years ago, maybe five. He wasn't sure. After the conversion he became the foreman for the crew who built the house.

"Charles hired me for that, couple years before he died."

"Charles?"

"Caspian."

We passed a sandblasted brick silo that had windows, a watchtower balcony and a shake roof.

"JT's place," Ray said. "We transformed that in our spare time. Never worked with curved glass windows before."

We veered away from the silo toward a huge two-story farmhouse where Ray parked his bike. Pieces of luggage were lined up along the porch railing. My duffel bag not among them.

"This house could use one of your bells too," Ray said as he swung back the screen door.

A rank smell hit me at the threshold.

"Get decent people!" Ray shouted as we entered. Reggae music throbbed through the floor above. Ray grabbed a shirt off a chair, wadded it up and tossed it up the stairs. "Hey, you pigs! Don't be leaving any mess for me to deal with!"

The music shut off and someone yelled down, "We're going to miss you Ray!"

"Good riddance!" he yelled back, then winced, "Who died?" He whiffed the air and went into the kitchen. "Good God!" He slammed the refrigerator door and hollered, "Nobody leaves until this fridge is cleared out of all your rotten shit!"

A screen door banged and a man shuffled into the kitchen from outside.

"That means you Spitzer," Ray said.

"What means me?"

"Cleaning this pit. I want this kitchen spotless."

"And if I don't, what are you going to do, kick me out?"

Ray stepped up chest to chest to the taller man. "I'll kick your ass."

"Ha! I'm outta here tomorrow. I don't have to answer to you or Julian anymore."

"The hell you don't!"

Ray stuck the heel of his left hand between his teeth and shoved the man back against the counter with his right.

The guy snorted and grabbed Ray's shirt with both hands. "You sure you want to do this?"

The smell of pent-up hostility filled the room. A smell I once wore like after-shave. My fingers curled into fists. A knee jerk reaction.

"God, is everybody on edge around here?" I said, not knowing that most of the workers were stir-crazy, having not been allowed to leave the property for over a year.

Ray bit down hard on the heel of his hand. His eyes burned with the ferocity of a mongrel dog defending its turf. It looked like the two were going to come to blows when a female voice cried out from behind me.

"Guys! Hey! Spitz, stop it!"

"He started it."

"Want to lose your pay over it?" she said. "Well, do ya?"

"Tough call," Spitzer said.

"Let it go," the woman urged.

Spitzer grinned and relaxed his grasp on Ray's shirt. That's all it took to defuse the face-off.

Ray eased the heel of his hand out of his mouth. A red arc of teeth marks dented the flesh.

"Spotless." Ray backed away from the man and nodded at the woman. "You too, April. Don't poison all the good work you've done by leaving this place a dump."

"We love you Ray," April said.

"Yeah, and I'll love you when you're all gone."

Ray walked me back into the living room and pointed to a futon. "You'll have to sleep down here tonight. Not to worry. You'll have your pick of rooms tomorrow when everybody splits. Could get loud later on with the partying and all, so if you need quiet there's a cot in the loft of the barn. That's where I used to sleep. Can't beat it."

"Do you know where my luggage is?"

"Right. I'll check on that." Ray swaggered to a window. "I'm in the trailer out back. Going to wash up now. In an hour or so, carts will shuttle people to the farewell bash at the big house. You can walk if you like."

The wretched smell in the kitchen drove me outside. I hiked up the hill to get an overview of the place. "The old Skogen farm," the cashier in Newgrange had described it to me. "Fifteen hundred acres of the prettiest land in the county. They bought out Rolf some years back. It'd been in the family for generations y'know, and he was nowhere near eager to sell. But here they come with a heap o' cash that got Rolf goin' all gooey in the head. He divorced Marsha. Sweet lady. Then moved away for a time only to come back sick and broke. Went into detox. Works for a trucking firm out of Oshkosh I hear."

Near the top of the hill I came upon a large circular slab of weathered concrete. It had a black and yellow bull's eye target painted on it and dandelions sprouting through its cracks. I figured it to be a helipad. The only thing missing was the helicopter, if there ever was one. I sat down in the center of the circle and thought about the old white-haired man in the photo I'd seen— Charles Caspian.

The Caspian Foundation.

I knew of it. Lucia had applied for a grant from them. They gave a lot to the arts.

So that's the money behind this place.

I racked my brain to recollect something about how Caspian made his millions. Then I lay back thinking about the 'vibrational trap' Tandre described. I pictured a clear gyroscopic ball clamped in the jaws of a giant mechanical paint can shaker. Other images followed. Things I'd seen in science fiction movies.

The orange sun melted into the horizon. In the distance a single engine plane purred a lonesome groan before fading away. Although worn down from the day, I felt curious and excited. I didn't want to leave now. I wanted to see this instrument Tandre had built.

A grasshopper fluttered past my head. Then all went quiet.

In the dream I'm neck deep in water, thrashing away to keep from drowning. All around me whirlpools spin. It takes all my strength to stay afloat. I'm not alone. To my left and right other people are being tugged down. We're all gulping water, trying to swim but the force is so strong it feels like a losing battle. An object appears floating out in front of me. It's a buoy bobbing in the water. "Swim to it," I tell myself. I pound my arms and legs, fighting furiously. It seems to take forever but finally I manage to reach the buoy and climb up, only to be tossed from side to side. As I begin to move with the buoy's rocking motion, the waves subside. The water clears. The teeter-tottering eases up and a calm comes over me, but only for an instant. Suddenly the water bulges in places and human heads break the surface, first one, then others, popping up all around me, water streaming down their faces. All their eyelids are stitched shut.

The beeping horns of golf carts woke me. It was already twilight. I hiked down the hill shaking off the nightmare. Ever since Lucia had me pay attention to my dreams I began seeing premonitions hidden within them. How a dream would puzzle together events in my past and present with those yet to come. The lasting image of the stitched eyelids I saw on the drowning faces didn't make any sense to me.

But it would.

Nearing the farmhouse, a cart pulled up.

"Need a ride?"

I got in and found Julian at the wheel.

"Well if it isn't Mr. Gandy," he said and we drove off. "I take it you heard the news about your project?"

"What news?"

"It's been cut."

"My bell?"

"Your bell, right. The bell's out."

"That's funny, Jean Tandre told me it was on."

"Well, you were told wrong. It's been scratched. And that's official."

"Official?"

"Don't you look at me like that. A lot of things get canceled around here." Julian bared his teeth. "You don't know this man. He's voracious."

Julian barked out a number of Tandre's demands and fantasies that included dredging a moat around the entire house, adding a zoo with elephants, giraffes, and zebras, building a hospice complex, a spa, and hiring a permanent symphony orchestra with a full choir.

"He's devoured the budget. The Greenhouse alone cost millions of dollars. And for what? It's a waste. If the man had his way the project would be bankrupt before it got off the ground. So don't feel alone. You can still come to the party. We'll deal with your things tomorrow."

As if I cared about a party.

We drove the rest of the way to the house in silence. He dropped me off near the front door. I stepped out of the cart feeling punched in the gut.

So be it. I didn't want to be here anyway. Too bad I do

*now. Still, I need to thank Tandre. After all, he may want
one of my bells on his next project.*

The entry was strung with tiny lights mimicking the
constellations of the zodiac. Musicians stood under the
lights playing a lively Irish drinking song. People mingled
about the grounds prattling on enthusiastically. I
definitely felt out of the groove.

"Hey dude." Ray appeared out of nowhere, hatless,
all cleaned up. His long hair tied back in a ponytail
exposing a shiny bald pate. "All the food's inside," he
said.

"Good, I haven't eaten all day."

"Appetite makes the best sauce."

As we skirted around clusters of people idly
sauntering toward the front door, I told him how I just
got axed.

"Say what?"

"They cut my bell," I said.

"Ha! Welcome to the Sylvia House."

Further on, Ray nudged me on the arm with a soft
fist.

"Hey listen, it ain't over 'til it's fuckin' over and
trust me, it ain't fuckin' over."

The front door was propped open and in the
illuminated lobby stood the roller-blade girl, welcoming
everybody.

"To the star of the show." Ray lifted his right arm and
handed the girl a single red rose. "For you, Sylvia."

She looked almost angelic wearing a halo of white
daisies on her head. She received the rose with an

infectious laugh that twinkled like the glass ceiling.

"Remember me?" I said.

At first she couldn't. I made a grasping gesture with my hand toward her wrist. That lit up the memory and she grimaced like a gremlin.

"Yeah, you remember."

Sylvia's coloring, along with photos, design plans, and the house model stood on display around the lobby. Someone took the pack off my back and walked it into the dining hall. Another person handed me a glass of champagne and directed me not to drink it yet.

Gudrun came over to us. She wrapped an arm around Ray and whispered something in his ear. Ray said something back. By their tone and somber expressions whatever they were talking about was anything but celebratory.

Soon everyone circled as Leonard Roe stepped to the center in a long black tailcoat and bowtie, lightly drumming his cane on the floor. He seemed taller than when he and Tandre clashed earlier in the architect's office.

"If you don't have a glass, please get one now," he said to those assembled.

In number there were only about 40 people. Yet their energy filled the lobby with an electric charge I could feel on my skin. And the roasting smells coming from the dining hall made my mouth water.

"This is a night I've been dreaming about for four years and seven months," Roe began. "Our goal of opening by the year 2000 has been reached with three months to spare. Plenty of time for us to head off any potential Y2K meltdowns. I wish first to acknowledge those who are not here."

Roe raised his glass and turned toward an easel with a cork panel studded with push-pinned photos of faces.

"To the teams of trade's people who did their part in the construction of this house and have gone on to other jobs. We thank them for their hard work and inspired effort. We will not forget them."

"Here, here!" people shouted.

"Now for those of you here tonight, what can I say? Moving your lives to this remote farm from far away. You've endured all manner of stress and strain."

"And sleep deprivation," someone interrupted.

"True."

"And confinement," another added.

"Yes, well, we are deeply grateful. Here's to you."

People whooped and applauded.

Someone started chanting, "JT, JT, JT." Others took up the chant, "JT, JT, JT."

Roe backed away as Jean Tandre stepped out of the circle to a barrage of applause. He was dressed in a common blue work shirt and a dark blue shop coat. No doubt playing the humble craftsman saluting his peers.

"For someone who never stops talking, I'm not one for speeches. The work speaks for itself. This house carries your touch, your care, and your craft. And that can never be taken away. Wherever you go from here you have a touchstone in you. And allow me to gush, a new wonder of the world."

Tandre walked over to the model of the house

displayed on a platform near the waterfall.

"I know most of you have been left in the dark. The rumors I've heard have kept me amused. Everything from astral travel to the fountain of youth. Well, tonight all rumors shall be put to rest. Tonight you will see the transcendent marvel of this house. I'll leave it to you to tell me its significance once you've seen it with your own eyes. As for me, my heart is full and thankful to you all."

Everyone emptied their glasses.

"Now allow me to make a toast," Tandre continued. "I wish to honor two people. Without them this wonder would not exist. Sylvia! Come out here and take a bow."

The girl catapulted to the center of the circle. The lobby erupted in cheers and hoots. She curtsied to the crowd, then veiled her mouth with both hands in embarrassed glee.

"Talk about keeping secrets," Tandre said. "Sylvie, you are an inspiration."

More champagne came around.

"And to Charles, Sylvia's father." Tandre gestured to an oil portrait of Charles Caspian. "The love he carries for his daughter has helped conquer the impossible. For this love we have been blessed beyond our lives."

"To Caspian," someone shouted and others joined in. "Yea, Caspian!"

"And one more," Tandre added. "Yes, its taken teams of people to build this place. Dare I count the number of tortured engineers littering the countryside. Yet pivotal to the challenge is a man who's done more than just sign your checks. He's also been a steady, loyal, and watchful eye throughout the adventure. I'm speaking about Charles' business partner." Tandre waved for Roe to step back out. "Leonard, please."

Interesting. Tandre toasting the person he just earlier called a hollow man.

Roe took two steps forward and dipped his head to scattered applause.

"Thank you everyone. And speaking of checks, please don't leave without seeing me tonight. Now a feast awaits us, so without further adieu…"

We filed into the dining hall. Empty tables I'd seen earlier now lined the walls covered with trays and horns of food from every corner of the world. Mounds of fresh figs, plums, almonds, mangoes and papaya. Each table featured a different region of food with its national flags suspended above. At the Asian station were glass-covered dishes of Peking duck, sweet and sour pork and green curry chicken. The Middle Eastern table had falafels and kebobs. At the American tables— steamed Texas barbeque ribs, sweet corn, baked potatoes, and smoked wild turkey.

While I piled my plate, Ray materialized at my side.

"Forget what you heard. The bell stays. JT knows how to clear the way. Stick around tonight. He'll call on you when it's time."

Finding a seat, I listened to the other people at my table jabbering about the girl, Sylvia.

"Well I won't miss little queenette," one said.

"No, but God, I'd love to have half her brain."

"I'd love to have half her trust fund."

"Spoiled brat."

"Cut her some slack. She lost her father. Has no mother. No kid friends. No TV even. And she lives in Weirdworld. Was your childhood like that?"

"My father ran off with his secretary when I was a baby. Was your childhood like that?"

"Still, no seven year old lives like this."

"Who is her mother? That's the big secret. Does anybody know?"

A swarthy looking man next to me gave me a nudge.

"No burgers here," he said with a thick Russian accent.

"Yeah," I said. "It's delicious. And I just got here today."

"Good timing," he said.

"That depends on who you talk to." I dug in, my mind treading in limbo. The on-again, off-again project was not going to work for me. But who was I to complain. I was being fed like a sultan.

Gorging away, I felt the sticky spotlight of someone's attention on me. I overheard a woman across the table ask the person next to her, "Who's the one with the eyes?" Between bites, I snuck a look at the woman. Ink-black hair in a black dress cleaved to the navel. I'm no psychic but I could sense that at some point later she'd be making herself known to me.

After the meal Tandre stood up and chimed his glass with the edge of a knife. "Everyone fully glutted? Ready for a treat? We're going to take a little after-dinner promenade. This ought to work off the pounds we just ingested. We're going to be hiking through the

Greenhouse. Then we'll crawl though a thirty-foot tunnel to what I call 'The Porch' for a little show and tell. Where's Gudrun?"

"Here!" Gudrun stood up.

"You all know Gudrun, our Icelandic home school teacher and all around therapist. She'll be with us should you need an ear, a story, or a hug."

We followed Tandre to a hidden door behind the reception counter. Julian and the rhino stood flanking the door, acting like nightclub bouncers, rejecting certain undeserving ones. The two took their direction from Roe, who leaned against the counter. He'd give a slight nod or shake of his head to let them know who to let in and who to weed out.

Fat chance Roe's going to allow me in to see Tandre's Porch, I'm thinking when a skirmish erupted. It was Spitzer, the guy Ray had confronted at the farmhouse, being wrangled out of the line and brutally wrestled to the floor by Julian and the rhino.

I edged around the fracas through the hidden door and caught up with the others down a hallway. Along the walls hung a procession of angel art by artists like Raphael and Bourgereau. There was a time I detested these depictions of winged cherubs whispering in the ears of goddesses. I'd gone the other direction in my youth as an artist. The only angel I ever created combined a butcher knife sharpened silver-bright and stuck into a thick chopping block between two downy swan wings. All lacquered up and shiny.

That was then.

The group collected for a minute at a pair of tall

glass doors that parted and we entered the lush, humid darkness of the Greenhouse.

"You are now entering a rain forest," Tandre explained. "More than an acre of trees and flora imported from the equator. It's the work of master forester, Yu Li. Unfortunately Mr. Li is in Hong Kong at the birth of a grandchild and could not be here tonight."

"Careful now," Roe called from the back of the line. "Follow the footlights, people."

High above the dark canopy of leaves stars blinked through the enormous glass dome. We crossed a stream that sloshed under a raised wooden bridge. The "oohs" and "ahhs" voiced by the others told me I wasn't the only first timer in there.

The forest path ended at a small, dimly lit clearing with a limestone floor. Tandre stood by an unassuming door and waited for everyone to gather around him. No longer the humble workman, he'd now transformed himself into an impresario.

"The conquest of space. America's got that down. All systems GO. Got the brains, the launch pads, and the power. And pots and pots of NASA money piled high as the moon. But when it comes to Death and the Afterlife, it's all systems NO. Bury the bodies and pray for the souls. We don't explore it. Don't fund it. Not on our senate floor. No, that's relegated to the occult province of candlelight séances and fortunetellers. And yet..."

Tandre paused to take in the people who faced him, fixed on his every word.

"What if I told you the Afterlife is through this door. Only a few steps away. And the dead, who are very much alive, can now speak with us. No mumbo jumbo. No Ouija boards or scary ghosts. But clear, face to face contact with those who've passed on. Your loved ones, your Einsteins, Socrates, the Who's Who of all time. Brace yourselves, my friends. The curtain is rising on the Afterlife. Right here in this house. Come see for yourself. Come see the mystery of mysteries revealed. No longer will Death be our enemy. From here on it will be our confidant."

That stirred up the crowd.

Tandre tapped some buttons on a keypad next to the door. I heard a hard click and whoosh sound as the door released.

"Sylvie, lead the way." Tandre held the door wide.

We funneled into a sizeable room. The 'mud room' Tandre called it. Long benches, stools and coat racks. At the far end, the mouth of a long, low tunnel beckoned like a vacuum. The tunnel was lit by tiny bead lights indented along both sides of its arched ceiling.

Following Sylvia's lead, people took off their shoes and got down on all fours. Some stared at the tunnel and balked. One woman stopped midway inside, petrified. Gudrun coaxed her back out.

Crawling the thirty feet on my knees reminded me of the roadside culvert near my home in San Francisco when I was a boy. My escape hatch from a loveless house to freedom and adventure at Baker Beach and Land's End.

At the far end of the tunnel we walked up a ramp edged with coin-sized footlights that gave the space the aura of dusk. The ramp sloped leisurely up to a deck that faced an immense clearing the size of an amphitheater with a bowled floor. A misty, egg-shaped cloud floated in the center, looking like those swarms of gnats that rise and fall in the summer sun.

Not everyone could fit on the deck, so a number of us clustered on the ramp. The air felt charged, not heavy or humid like the rain forest, but compressed, as if the space contained double the molecules. Instantly I became aware of the acoustics. A rich vibrancy with the barest trace of an echo, and a subtle, low riding reverberation like the slow drum roll of a tympani underfoot.

After my eyes adjusted to the dark, I could see Tandre standing at a podium where the deck jutted into the clearing. He was speaking but the jostling of people drowned out his words. Finally the crowd settled so we could hear him.

"… and the ancient Egyptians knew this thousands of years ago. Their pyramids were not burial chambers for pharaohs like many historians believe. They were communication bridges to other dimensions, other worlds. Although this Porch is a far cry from the great pyramids of Giza, it produces one of those etheric levels. A soul communication system to be precise. I'll spare you the metaphysics. As they say, seeing is believing. Sylvie, call your father."

Tandre stepped aside for the girl to approach the podium. She stood on her tiptoes and belted out, "Charles Caspian. I call for Charles Caspian."

Heads turned as little veins of light unfurled from the egg of mist followed by prismatic bands of color— pastel magentas and phosphorescent greens. Like photographs I'd seen of the aurora borealis.

Pushing forth from the cloud, the facial features of a man clarified. It looked like a stippled portrait painted in the pointillist style. Only, this one came to life.

"Caspian," people gasped around me.

"It's my Daddy!" Sylvia proudly shouted.

"Sylvia, my dear." Caspian spoke, and everyone hushed. All except for one.

"Hologram," the person called out.

"No, I am not a hologram," Caspian said, hearing it too. "I am the astral body of Charles Caspian. The one responsible for all your hard labor and headaches. Some of you know me. Many do not. I cannot see most of you because of where you stand. But before we conclude I would like each of you, one at a time, to step up to the lighted mount where my daughter is standing so I can thank you. For now I will just say hello."

He looked younger than the man in the photo I'd seen. But the face was unmistakable. His features had all the articulation of a living person, only more fluid. His eyes gave a mirror-like quality like pools of clear water. The lips on his face moved, but his voice sounded more detached, not coming so much from the mouth as from all around us in the space.

Right away I questioned my perception.

How can this be happening? Where's the light coming from? Must be a trick. Some kind of spectral illusion.

I looked past the others who stood mesmerized by the vision. I scanned the walls for a projection booth. Any light source other than the footlights. But all around was darkness.

"A window has been opened between two worlds," Caspian said. "And you are its first beholders. Jean? Where are you?"

Tandre stepped alongside Sylvia.

"Yes, Charles."

"I poured all my faith in this man, as well as my worldly wealth. This crazy dreamer with his rowdy, unpredictable reputation. And I a dreamer as well. What a gamble, eh Leonard? Leonard does not like gambles. For those of you who may have already heard the story, please indulge me. Like you always should with those who've passed away, or else we will haunt you."

No one said a thing. They simply stared, spellbound.

"I'm joking," Caspian said.

No one laughed.

"Now, tracking Jean down was as much an ordeal as designing and constructing this house. I'm a dying man and I'm globetrotting to Geneva and Paris meeting with him and he's toying with me like a cat with a cornered mouse. Finally, I pin him down back at his home in New York and..." Caspian's voice distorted momentarily then came back. "...to create a bridge that reaches the shore of the dead. A bridge I can cross again and again to visit my daughter and see her grow after I've passed on. And for her to see me and to know her father is there for her. Well, here I am. And there is Sylvia. Not only can I see her and others, we can..." Again Caspian's voice became jumbled.

"Apologies," Tandre interrupted. "The instrument

still has a few audio bugs to sort out."

Caspian's voice soon returned. "The fiddle-faddle as Ray would say. Right, Ray?"

"You got it," Ray said.

"Glad you're staying around, Ray," Caspian said. "Now, let's hear from you people."

Sylvia spoke first.

"Daddy…"

"Yes, sweetheart."

"Dingo's gone."

"Your doggie?"

"We can't find him."

"I'm sorry, sweetheart," Caspian said. "He'll turn up. Now, if you would my dear, since we talk every day, please let others speak. Most of them will be leaving soon."

"Will you look for Dingo on your side?"

"I wouldn't know quite where to look."

Roe turned to the crowd, raised his hand and spread his fingers. "Five minutes for questions."

"Ah, the timekeeper has spoken," Caspian said. "Mustn't upset him. Your questions please."

"Speak out loud and clear," Tandre directed. "So Charles can hear you."

"What is death like?" Someone asked among the crowd crammed on the deck.

"Death is very much alive with abundant activity. And although I am only at one station, I can say this, so far I haven't seen any angels playing harps on clouds or red-horned Satan's scampering around."

Caspian waited for a response. None came.

"Then again, the Afterlife is not all goodness and light. The adage, 'as above, so below' is quite true. There is as much work to be done here as on the physical plane. So, I would instruct you all to let go the belief that when you pass away you're going to lay back on some happy hammock for your soul. That is a comfortable lie. Work and learning do not cease unless you wish to cease altogether. Better to wish the departed that they continue to grow and evolve than to rest in peace."

The woman next to me lifted her arm. "I have a question. Is it true that we re-experience our life after we die?"

"The Great Remembering, indeed. Personally, I am in the midst of my review. It is not a trifling matter and for me quite agonizing. Your choices and the consequences of your choices and actions are acutely experienced with uncompromising clarity. As it must be. How else are souls ever to stop repeating transgressions in the physical world?"

Caspian paused momentarily as if expecting another question. Then he continued.

"I'm also learning about the significance in how one dies. How conscious you are when you cross over is of great importance. Trauma, cruelty and some of the darker emotions will affect the tenor of your entry, the level you reach and the work ahead."

Again Caspian stopped. No one stirred.

"We could spend many of your days discussing this," he said. "Years in fact. And soon we shall. For myself, much of what I'm given to do is preparing other souls for this re-connection with your world. There has been such a rift between the physical and spiritual dimensions and sensing the surprise on your faces, well, it is no different on this side. It is quite like being invited to a large family reunion, and you all know about family reunions."

Roe waved to a couple people to move up to the podium.

Looks like some people made reservations to speak to the dead.

"Mind you, there are many on this side clamoring to re-unite," Caspian went on. "And there is a great deal of work to be done so that the underpinnings of this bridge never collapse again."

"How do we know this is not a hoax," someone hollered. "Some kind of masquerade and you're working levers behind a curtain?"

"That's the question I would ask," Caspian replied. "And I can swear to you there are no tricks or gimmicks. What you are seeing is not a projection. But truly there's only one way to prove it, and that is to bring through someone you know who has passed on. The only condition is that it is someone within reach. A relative, say. Or a close friend. Do you know such a person?"

The man squirmed, no doubt feeling self-conscious with all eyes on him.

"My mother," he said.

"Then, by all means, call her name," Caspian said.

"Her name is Martha Enright."

"No, say it over here in the thingie," Sylvia said.

The group made a path for the man to reach the podium. Sylvia coached him. He leaned forward and summoned his mother.

"Martha Enright. I call for Martha Enright."

Everyone turned to the cloud. Caspian's face atomized into particles of mist, then gradually reconstituted into the face of a woman. She appeared to be about forty, with short-cropped hair and bangs.

"Someone calls for me?"

"That's my mom," the man stuttered to the people around him.

"Bobby? Bobby!" she bubbled. "Oh, Bobby my dear, just look at you. You're a man, a grown man. You have a moustache."

The man looked physically shaken. This was no plant. He gripped the edge of the podium for support as he shared with his mother how his father raised him and his older brother in the Virginia house where she once lived. How his father re-married. His older brother became a building contractor, and he himself works as a gardener here at the house.

"I still plan to finish school."

"You are young, with a long life ahead. What you do is not as important as who you become, and the voice you chose to follow. You can follow the voice of weakness that says, 'I am less.' Or the voice of strength that says, 'I am more.' "

Bobby began weeping, which incited sobs in others.

"Are people sad?" his mother said. "We can speak openly with you now. Be happy." She looked back at her son. "I must allow time for others. Bobby. I hope we can talk again soon."

The woman's warm, contented face atomized into the mist.

"She died when I was thirteen," Bobby explained, wiping his eyes on his sleeve.

As he back-stepped into the shadows a young woman approached the podium. It was Camie, the receptionist. She nodded to Sylvia and to Jean Tandre before facing the Afterlife cloud, her hands clasped at her chest.

"Amal Balarbi. I call for Amal Balarbi."

Everyone turned to look at the cloud except me. I wanted to see Camie's expression the moment the person she was calling appeared— to see if her reaction was genuine.

Camie's lips spread into a smile. Her dark eyes lit up. She threw her arms open, embracing the face that manifested in the cloud.

"My grandfather!" she exclaimed.

Her grandfather's eyes squinted intently at Camie. Then he started talking in a foreign language no one understood.

"He is speaking the language of my home country," Camie said. "I will try to translate. First he asked me, 'Who calls for him?' And I answered, "It is your grand-daughter, Camilie." Now he says... "Camilie, you are a woman and your eyes still shine as bright as the child I knew. Do you remember the old caravan song I would sing to you?

Hear the camels stir and grumble
Smell the tea steaming on the fire
Time to rise and roll your blanket
Tie your rope to the caravan
Yesterday the wind was fierce
And filled the sky with sand
Today brings us the morning star
And we shall reach the well."

And that was it. Camie's grandfather disappeared into the cloud without a goodbye. Not that he needed to say anything more. People buzzed around me. Some clapped their hands.

Tandre quieted things down. "Go ahead," he said to Camie.

"My grandfather, Amal Balarbi, was a scholar and translator who traveled all over North Africa and the Middle East. He visited our home when I was a little girl and shared stories about his journeys. He made a dear and lasting impression. Thank you for letting me speak to him."

"Thank you," some shouted back.

As Camie left the podium, another woman stepped up. By the hoots of the crowd, a popular one.

"Yea, Louise!"

People edged closer to the railing on the porch. The woman waved her hands to quiet everyone. She said she wanted to see her father who was killed eight years ago on Special Forces duty weeks before the advent of the Gulf War. She called his name. Nothing happened.

She repeated the name. Still, no shift in the cloud. Tandre had the woman try different name combinations along with the man's rank. The cloud pulsed with every name, but no face formed.

"What's going on?" Louise asked Tandre, puzzled. "Why isn't he coming?" She looked at the cloud, choking back tears. "What does this mean? Is my father still alive?"

Tandre shrugged, set his hands on her shoulders and gently rotated her body at the podium.

"One more time," he said.

The woman collected herself and called out her father's name again. All heads turned to the cloud as a breathless silence filled the space.

In the hush of the moment the pain of losing Lucia came crushing in on me. I tried to bury the flashback of her car accident with a vision of her buoyant face— there on the flat, warehouse rooftop of my studio, lying in the porcelain claw-foot bathtub we'd rescued from a vacant lot. She was sipping yerba mate tea. Her legs bent up at the knees. A book in her lap. She loved South American writers. She said they wrote with all six senses.

Shaking off the memory, I looked back at the cloud. Nothing had changed. The woman slumped at the podium. The whereabouts of her father a lingering mystery.

"Let's call Elvis!" Someone broke the ice. This brought a scattering of nervous laughs and jeers. Then a man walked up to the podium. The guard I'd seen outside in the garden when I first arrived. A burly man with a flat nose and jowly cheeks who reminded me of a bulldog. He asked to see his daughter, Janie.

The mist took on a burnt orange tint and the face of a young woman fleshed out with a sour frown.

"Janie, wow. There you are." The man nodded in recognition.

"What the hell do you want?" Janie's agitated voice jarred the space.

The man looked around at the crowd. "That's my Janie, alright."

"I said what do you want!"

"Just want to know you're okay." The man smiled. A vain attempt to appear upbeat.

"No, I'm not okay. And what do you care?"

"What do you mean? Of course I care."

"That's a lie! You were never there for me. Never, never, never."

"I did all I could. I had to work y'know." The man shifted his feet.

"You weren't there when I told you I wanted to divorce Gary. 'Stick it out,' you said."

"I said that?"

"I remember your every word. 'Stick it out, Janie. Weather the storm.' Don't you stand there and deny it! I told you how scared I was. How he slapped me around. And how I wanted out of the marriage. I was pregnant for Chrissakes! And did you listen? No. 'Every marriage goes through its up and downs,' you said. Well how far down is murder?"

"What? What murder?"

"You think it was suicide? That I would ever harm

my baby?"

"What are you talking about?"

"What I'm talking about is that asshole killed me and made it look like a drug overdose."

"Gary? No. They looked into all that. You left a note."

"I never wrote no note."

The man's face paled. "What? No. Oh, Jesus, Janie, no. I-I don't know what to say."

"Well don't say you're sorry. I'm the one who's sorry. I'm sorry I ever married the son of a bitch."

"How the hell was I to know?"

"Well, you know now! And if you really care about me like you say, you'll find Gary and stick your hunting knife into his heart a hundred times. Promise me that, father. Promise me you'll track him down and kill him! And I'll be here to greet him... on my terms."

The crowd gasped.

Tandre stepped up and called for Caspian.

Angered and embarrassed by the confrontation, the man shoved his way through the people to get off the deck of the Porch, grumbling in denial, "She's wrong. It wasn't like that."

Sylvia shouted, "Daddy's coming back!"

"Did something happen?" Caspian said, sensing the turmoil.

"Charles can't see what goes on in his absence," Tandre explained.

"A bit of trouble?"

"Hard truths, Charles."

"Hmm, like I said, not everything on this side is rosy. Far from it. And yet, that can change now. We have broken through to the light beyond the grave."

Roe piped in, "Time for one more."

Heads dipped. No one volunteered.

"Anyone?"

Dead silence.

"Perhaps that's enough for now," Caspian said. "Congratulations to all of you. We are re-uniting the worlds. It is a blessed occasion. I trust you will treat this house and your experience with reverence and respect. Now please, one at a time, step up to where Sylvia is standing. Tell me your name so I can thank you personally."

People jammed their way up to the podium. But Caspian never finished thanking everyone. His voice became choppy and incoherent.

Flustered, Tandre stopped it all. "Sorry, folks. There's never been this many people in here. It could be what's gumming up the gears."

As Caspian's face vanished away into beads of mist, my body contracted. I realized that I'd just blown an unbelievable chance to see Lucia.

The man beside me shouted out to no one in particular, "Not me, man. I don't want to see any of 'em. Let them bygones be bygones. That's what I say."

Tandre quieted everyone. "Someone just asked me if it's possible to talk to the Virgin Mary or Buddha. At this point we can only make contact by personal association, with relatives and people we've known and touched. The instrument works by vibratory familiarity. Personal and emotional attachments assert the strongest connections."

Roe jumped on that.

"Of course we'll endeavor to expand the scope of association. In time we hope to contact all the great ones who ever lived. Imagine hearing history from those who actually lived it." Roe pointed his cane at the tunnel. "But right now we need to return to the celebration. Dessert is about to be served, and we'll try to answer more of your questions. Julian, why don't you guide everyone out."

I started to follow the people when Ray took me aside.

"Stay here, JT wants to talk."

The Porch emptied leaving only Tandre and Roe in a heated exchange near the podium.

"No! No more stalling!" Roe fumed. He thumped his cane on the floor as if planting a flag. "There is nothing to discuss. Fix the audio reception and get me those plans!"

He brushed me aside and stamped off the Porch.

Tandre combed his beard with his fingers until he heard Death's Door swoosh shut. Then he waved me up to the deck.

As I climbed the ramp I heard a high-pitched wail of distress to my right. A spark of light flashed with a crackling sizzle. When I looked to see what it was, I saw nothing, just blackness. *Weird*, I thought, but let it go and stepped up onto the deck of the Porch.

The semi-circular podium was part of an extensive audio console composed of vector scopes, waveform monitors, rows of knobs and switches. Most of it outside my grasp.

"Gandy, my apologies for all the mix up. I want to talk to you about how we make the bell happen, but first I need to take care of something if you don't mind."

Tandre leaned forward at the podium.

"Charles Caspian. I call for Charles Caspian."

Like sunlight under the surface of the sea, the cloud undulated with filaments of pastel colors. I moved over next to Tandre to see Caspian's face straight on. From the front more of his astral body was visible, the misty particles tapering out of sight below the man's chest.

"Sorry to bother you, Charles," Tandre began. "I wouldn't have called you again if it wasn't important. As you know, my work here is almost done. However, in completing some of the details of the house, Leonard and I, well, we've come to the impasse I suspected. I fear harm may be done if we do not confront it now."

"Where is Leonard?"

"He refused to join us. He feels it's a mistake to bring you into these affairs."

"Who is this with you?"

"Oh, forgive me. This is Gandy. Maker of magical bells."

"Pleased to meet you."

"In fact, Gandy's project is an example of a number of budget cuts and rigid decrees that have caused me to question Leonard's intentions."

"I see."

"Perhaps I should have brought this up when I first felt there was a problem."

"This is a fragile situation, Jean. It's best we clear it up as soon as possible. Bring Leonard here at my request."

"Very well." Tandre looked over at me. "Do you wish to stay?"

"Oh, by all means," Caspian said before I could answer. "You can tell me about these bells of yours."

Tandre left me there alone to describe my bells to the disembodied man.

"A harmonic bell. I like it," Caspian said. "You know, in olden times they had what was called the 'passing bell,' which they rung at one's death bed to declare the passing of the soul from the body. So, it is only fitting to hang a bell here at the house."

"Just one problem, the bell's been canceled," I said.

"I see. Well, there must be a logical reason."

I didn't know where to go with that. There was an awkward stretch of silence where neither of us said anything. Then my curiosity took over.

"Can I ask you a question?"

"Of course."

"Earlier you said you were at one station. What did you mean by that?"

"Quite simply, there are a number of states of being, or stations, beyond the physical plane. I am currently at one of them."

"You mind telling me what they are?"

"You wish to know the stations of the Afterlife?"

"I do."

Caspian looked at me for the longest time before speaking.

"Typically, when your body dies you enter a transitory phase where you still carry a sense of your physicality. It's a state where many souls get stuck not believing they're truly dead and are unable to move on. Hopefully you'll be met by loved ones who can help guide you through this troublesome transition."

"Go to the light."

"Exactly."

"So, where do souls go from there?"

"Understand, we are speaking about a circuitous etheric system. In the most rudimentary of terms, there are five stations, or Afterlife states, with multiple offshoots between them. In the first station your soul works to detach from your physical body more completely. Your life experience and the wisdom you've earned pass on to the second station of the etheric realm."

Caspian looked at me as if waiting to see if his words were sinking in.

"Where...?"

"Where you find out if you learned what you came in to learn and if you accomplished what you came in to accomplish."

"Your karma."

"Your growth. This is also where the soul can repair from the fear of its body dying and not carry that fear into its next life."

"Souls feel fear?"

"Very much so. Realizing that your life is more than a physical body is not as easy as it sounds. Let me be the first to confess. Very few humans know who they are as a soul. Do you?"

"Do I...?"

"Do you know who you are as a soul without your body?"

"Can't say I do."

"You're not alone. And yet having your identity so tightly tied to the physical body can make shedding it an enormous challenge."

"So... how can we begin to know who we are as a soul with and without a body?"

"You will need to be more connected with your soul to know that. And you will, we hope, when we open this bridge between the worlds."

"You hope?"

"Nothing is certain."

"I get that. So, then..."

"Then?"

"There's a third station?"

Caspian didn't answer right away. His face softened. He appeared to be seeking the answer, or wondering if he should share it with me.

"I'm looking for a way to express this without offending any sensibilities. You see the third station is where your beliefs can cage you. It is where you may find yourself frozen in a false state of being that blocks you from graduating further. So, be careful how fervently you grip onto your precious beliefs, they can act like spells and enslave you even after you've passed on. Do you understand?"

"Like believing in the existence of heaven and hell?"

"Precisely."

I didn't think I had any hard and fast beliefs. Not that Caspian gave me a second to ponder it.

"You may not know until you collide with them," he said.

"Got it. And there's a fourth station?"

"The Fourth, as I'm informed, is where you meet your true self. If you're ready. Here again, I'm learning that many become so frightened at seeing their true selves they freeze up and return."

"Return where?"

"Reincarnate."

"Back to a physical body?"

"Right back to the school yard. As I mentioned to the group, dying is not a trifle matter."

"Okay, and from there? You said there were five stations."

"I'm no one to speak about the fifth station even if I had the words. And allow me to advise you. Be careful with your demands to know everything this instant. Such knowledge has its own timing. And greed will solidify a soul."

I felt disciplined. Still, I wanted to know more.

"There is much to learn," he went on as if reading my thoughts. "And through this soul transmission instrument it will now be possible. No longer will the departed drink from the mythical River Lethe before being born."

"The river what?"

"The River of Forgetfulness."

The suction sound of Death's Door rushed up the tunnel onto the Porch. Someone was coming. But I didn't stop. I still had questions for the dead man.

"How is this transmission done?"

"By energetic alignment. As for the mechanism, you'll have to ask the vibrational architect. And I doubt Jean will tell you."

"Why here?" I asked.

"Here?"

"Wisconsin. Way out in nowhere."

"Being in a remote place has its advantages. We needed to be assured of security both political and public. We would not want to build in a location that might be threatened by hostile forces, fanatical groups, the military, perish the thought, or even the nosey media. Not for the first house."

"There'll be more?"

"Many. Like public libraries. A place where you can check in on an old friend. This is merely a prototype. Someday it will be a shrine."

Footsteps approached. Tandre returned to the podium, alone.

"Charles," he said.

"Where's Leonard?"

"He objects to mixing business with the celebration. He said he will speak to you tomorrow on the subject."

"That will be fine. Tell him I understand and that I wish to talk with both of you together."

"He mentioned some 'money people' coming here tomorrow."

"Oh?"

"Investors of some sort."

"I had not heard."

"Not surprised. I'll tweak the receptor plates in the morning."

"Good. Work out the bugs. And we will have our talk. And you..." Caspian addressed me. "Bring in your harmonic bell. It appears we could use a little harmony around here."

Caspian's face dissolved.

"That's some instrument you built," I said to Tandre as we made our way down the ramp.

He didn't respond. His mind pre-occupied.

Hunkering at the mouth of the tunnel I glanced back at the misty cloud and its beehive of souls buzzing to be heard. It looked so innocent there for the phenomenal power it held. A healing power. And treacherous all the same.

"Your late arrival is most auspicious, my friend," Tandre's voice resounded in the tunnel. "Watch your head."

At the time, I took it as a warning for me not to bonk my skull against the ceiling of the tunnel. Now I know different.

"What's the significance of the tunnel?" I asked, sitting in the mudroom, pulling on my cowboy boots.

Tandre looked over at the hole in the wall.

"I like to think of it as mandatory reverence. A birth canal that forces one to bow to the Infinite Spirit. Truth be told, I forgot to create an entrance to the space. So, I punched a hole. Anything larger would upset the dynamics. Unfortunately, the frail and handicapped are unable to attend. That shall be remedied. Always something to solve."

While we walked back through the rain forest, I peppered Tandre with questions about the dead people he'd seen. Who they were, what they shared, the secrets they revealed, and any truths they set straight.

He was hesitant at first. I kept pressing.

"Leonard urged me to invite descendants of famous people to visit," he said. "You see, once a deceased appears in the cloud it registers an imprint. Think of it like the soul's phone number. From then on the personal connection or bloodline does not need to be present. Anyone can step up to the podium and bring that person back by calling their full name."

"You're saying you can slowly collect like a Rolodex of dead people that you can call on again and again?"

"Yes. Of course, I initially sought out great artists. Relatives of people like Picasso and Frank Lloyd Wright. But out of fear, dread, or utter disbelief all of the descendants, to a person, declined to speak to their ancestors. And this stubbornness goes both ways. It took countless tries before my estranged father would even speak a word to me from the other side."

Tandre shut the Greenhouse doors behind us and we continued along the hallway back to the lobby.

"They say you can't take it with you, but we do," he said. "We take all our crap with us. Like you just saw. There's a dark side of Heaven, Gandy. Maybe in time the dead will teach us how to die and then we can stop hauling all our lies and pain and dumping it over there like it's some God almighty landfill."

As we approached the door at the end of the hall, I

heard the murmurings of voices in the lobby.

Tandre sighed, "I hate farewells. Must be why I'm so obsessed with contacting those who've died. Never have to say goodbye."

He pressed a large red button beside the door.

"So, do I begin working on the bell?"

"At once," Tandre said. The door slid open. "Start tomorrow. Ray is there to help. Whatever you need."

We stepped into the lobby and someone shouted, "Here's to JT. The bastard did it!"

People whooped, whistled, and clapped their hands over their heads, only to be silenced by a woman bursting out of the crowd, red-faced and pissed as hell, pointing a poison finger at Tandre.

"Now you've done it, you fat foreign devil! Now you crossed the line! There are reasons we're not allowed to meddle with the Divine. But no, you have to defy God and violate his sacred plan."

Tandre listened and shook his head. "I beg to differ."

People shuffled back a step, giving the woman elbow room. And she took it, raving.

"This is a crime, a holy crime! And you, you greedy, puppet of evil, you're pulling heaven down to hell!"

"April, shut the fuck up!" Ray shouted.

"No! I will not! And all this time I thought we were building a refuge, a sanctuary of healing."

"May I say something?" Tandre tried to squeeze in a word.

"Don't you see what's happening here?" April turned her back on Tandre in an effort to mobilize the others. "Open your eyes, people. Brenda. Richard.

Listen to me. Don't think for a minute this is a 'blessed occasion.' This is sorcery, wicked and wrong. I know it. And I know I'm right. But I need your help. All of you. We must stop this now. Help me. We've got to shut this house down before it's too late!"

"No you don't!" Sylvia squirted between legs of the crowd and stormed up to April waving a cookie in her little hand, "You can't stop me from seeing my Daddy!"

"Sorry to pop your balloon little princess, but your Daddy's under the spell of that necromancer over there."

"April…" Tandre edged closer to her but Julian and the rhino intervened. They elbowed him back and snatched April by both arms.

"Let go of me! It's Jean Tandre you need to take away!"

"Gorno! Stop that!" Tandre roared. "Let us talk this out!"

But they didn't stop. They dragged the enraged woman out of the lobby and down the south corridor into darkness.

"Gorno! Julian! Bring her back here!"

Too late. She was gone, thrashing and shrieking. Leaving a chill in the air.

Looking at the faces of those around me I could see doubts forming in their minds. 'Maybe April's on to something. Maybe we've broken a spiritual boundary and blindly, egotistically, unleashed the demons of Hell.'

April was right about one thing, a threshold had definitely been crossed. And everyone who'd been on the Porch that night would never be quite the same again.

Murmurs rumbled the air of the lobby. Roe stood by the door to the dining hall, a walkie-talkie clutched to his mouth.

Tandre smoldered for a moment, then lifted his arms and let out a deep sigh. "Sorry friends. That didn't have to happen. We knew this portal would test our fundamental beliefs and fantasies."

"Blew my mind, man!" someone hollered.

"That, too. I will say this in response to April's accusation— the only hell I know is being disconnected from the ones I love. And it is that love that built this house."

"Ta da!" Sylvia jumped into Tandre's arms and the room lightened back up.

"That lady called you bad things," Sylvia said.

"Yes." Tandre nodded. "April likes her fear far too much."

The girl bit into her cookie.

"So my friends," Tandre appealed to the gathering, "If anyone else has a grievance or something they need to get off their chest, come talk to me."

A finger poked me in the shoulder.

"Hey you," Sylvia said.

"Hey you back."

"What do you do?"

"I make bells?"

"Bells? Make one for me?"

"I did."

"You did?"

"Well, for your house," I said.

"Show me."

"How's tomorrow?"

"Okay." She slid down out of Tandre's arms and ran off, disappearing among the crowd.

A plate of cheesecake was set in my hand. More champagne was poured. People chattered away, relating their experience.

"God, that was sooo strange …"

"… and I got the Marx Brothers on my mother's side of the family. Be wild to talk to them."

As I made my way to the dining hall to fetch my backpack, I noticed Gudrun sitting at one of the banquet tables holding hands with two hysterical people. I gave them a wide girth as I circled the room, my pack nowhere to be seen. Thinking they may have stashed it in the kitchen, I entered the fray of caterers and clean up. Seeing all the leftovers, I scavenged some cloth napkins and folded pieces of cake, ribs, French bread, and slices of smoked turkey into them. Memories of leaner and meaner days came to mind as I stuffed the pockets of my shop coat.

Walking out into the dining hall I nearly collided with the woman who had eyeballed me earlier at the banquet.

"Looking for this, hon?"

She held my canvas backpack in her arms.

"As a matter of fact."

"You're a newcomer."

"This is true," I said.

"I saw you standing there with the necromancer. So, what's your story?"

"Just your basic doorbell maker." I reached for the backpack, but she held it tight.

"Door bell?"

I could tell she was bombed by the way her head bobbled around while she yammered non-stop.

"Now why is it I don't believe you? Oh well. Hey, some light show in there, huh? I felt like a paparazzi of the dead. And April, my God, I could've strangled the self-righteous bitch. But hey, that's the kind of feedback you're going to get when you play God. Oh, oops, you're not a friend of April's are you?"

She didn't wait for me to answer.

"No, of course not, you just got off the boat. I love these people who cruise in here after the war is over and everything seems all bliss and peaches and they don't see the battle wounds and basket cases."

"I have no illusions."

"Oh, there they are— one blue and one green. Wow. I gotta say those eyes of yours are unreal. I mean are they like tinted contact lenses or are you some kind of exotic?"

I wrestled the pack away from her and slung it over my shoulder. "Excuse me, but I've got work to do."

"Work? Now? Hey, don't run away." She latched onto my hand. "Some calluses you got there. Let me have a look at that. I read palms y'know." She lifted my hand into the light. "What are all these welts and scars?"

"Hot slag. From welding."

"Honey, honey, honey, lotion, lotion, lotion." She turned my hand over to look at the palm. "Ooo, here we go. Name's Wanda, by the way. Wanda Lutz. I'm one of the sweatshop artists here. And you are?"

I didn't say.

"Well, these hands have worked like the devil and... oh my God, what do we have here?" She slid a fingertip along my life line. "Man, you've got one serious interruption..."

"Gotta go." I jerked my hand free.

In the lobby Tandre was flirting with Camie the receptionist, a girl half his age. Pushing my shoulders through the people I could feel someone staring at me. When I reached the front door I glanced back to catch Leonard Roe handing out white envelopes with me dead in his sights. A stocky woman in a lab coat stood on tiptoes, talking in his ear. I figured her for the resident nurse once I realized the party hat she wore was actually a medical mask.

Outside, I sucked in a deep breath as people shuffled in and out of the house awestruck, drunk, or both.

What a send-off for these workers. Boggle their minds and bid them goodbye.

Taking a tape measure out of my backpack I sized up the dimensions of the gable entry. The height afforded enough room for the bell, but while I jotted the measurements in my tablet, I realized a fatal flaw in the plan. The gable was cantilevered off the wall. Far too flimsy to carry the bell. I'd need four beefy posts or columns and a strong beam to bear the weight. I considered looking for Ray to tell him, but it wasn't the time. I finished my calculations and walked away from the house, my mind swirling. I waved off a cart and hiked up the hill to the workshop on foot.

Here and there solitary shadows lurked, watching everything that moved. I took them to be security.

After what I saw on the Porch they'll need the National Guard to protect this place. And where are the video surveillance cameras? The only one I've seen was at the guard shack at the front gate.

My thoughts raced as I climbed the hill. Visions and forebodings churned in my brain of the social and political repercussions of the Porch. Some beliefs and legends were bound to bite the dust. Crazies would be coming out of the woodwork to descend on the place. And in the wrong hands the instrument could let loose the barbarians of old and their agents of carnage and genocide. Pictures I didn't see hanging on their wall of angels.

On the other hand, I thought, if governed properly, who knows, there might be a chance Tandre's instrument could sustain an enlightened communion beyond this life. A future where departed souls participated in deciding world affairs. Where Jesus had a talk show on television. Where dead victims, like Janie, named their perpetrators in a court of law. And where one's true love could never be ripped forever from your life by a car accident on a foggy mountain road.

What I'd give to see Lucia. And damn if I missed my chance. Or did I? Caspian asked to see the bell, didn't he? I can ask Tandre if I can see Lucia when we bring the bell to the Porch. If it will fit through the tunnel that is. Shit, I didn't think of that.

"Lucia," I spoke her name out loud in the clear night. And glancing up at the stars it came to me.

I'd even forego my fee to see her. That's it! Give up my fee. They're so worried about their precious budget. I'll give them the bell in exchange for seeing Lucia.

Deal.

The thought of seeing her gave me a surge of energy. I found the light switches in the barn and drew up the specs for the entry: four 12-inch diameter columns to support the gable and a cross beam to hang the bell. No steel. A manual, hardwood striker. Not a ramrod. Make the head spherical. Hang it tastefully next to the front door from a brass bracket. Keep it simple.

Carts came and went up the road dropping revelers off at the farmhouse. A lone saxophone blew a raspy blues tune. People howled and laughed by a snapping fire. The moon rose, bulging full and white in the sky. Its cool light spilled into the barn through the high, clerestory windows.

Using the lumber I found outside the barn, I assembled a makeshift framework to hang the bell for Caspian. I located a heavy-duty furniture dolly that could roll the bell and scaffold pieces through the tunnel. Then I cleaned up my mess and took the scraps of lumber outside. The party at the farmhouse was still going strong. More musicians had joined the sax player with guitar and harmonica. Some drummed sticks against rounds of firewood. Wanda and others danced by the high flames that flapped from the fire pit. Seeing them party made my decision easy. No futon on the floor of the farmhouse for me. I would sleep in the loft of the barn.

Tomorrow, check in with Tandre. And Ray. Get Ray to help bring the bell down to the house with the ATV.

Exhausted, I shut off all the lights except the general shop light. I went to the restroom where a small, chipped mirror hung by a nail over the sink. The mirror reflected a haggard, warlock-looking face. A mat of brown hair uncut for months framed a pair of glassy, blood-shot eyes, hollow cheeks and a crooked nose broken many years before in a brawl that ended my stint in high school.

Next to the mirror someone had printed on the wall with a black marker:

ROE, ROE, ROE YOUR BOAT
ALL THE WAY TO HELL
MERRILY, MERRILY, MERRILY, MERRILY
EVERYONE'S EXPENDABLE

Climbing the stairs to the loft, a flash of light caught my eye through the barn windows. It came from the upper story of Tandre's silo— a single beam darting about. I thought nothing of it at the time. I slung my shop coat over the rail and fell asleep in my clothes.

The dream began in a dark cave that morphed into the Porch. But I'm not on the ramp or at the podium.

I'm out in the clearing, suspended in the air, moving toward the cloud. I can see it up close. A mist of fine droplets free-floating in space. They circulate in a mobius pattern. Each one a tiny, pearly ball, spinning around. Their spinning gives off chime-like sounds. Something tells me the little balls are alive. I watch them shift their pattern, moving in unison like a school of fish. Then they cluster in places, shaping something. A face. A person's face. "Oh, let it be Lucia," I say or think, urging Lucia's face to appear— her high cheek bones, her night-black eyes. "Lucia, Lucia... it's me," I say, my heart booming louder than my voice. "It's me, Joe." Her lips curve up in a warm, humming smile. I close in and press my lips into hers. The droplets tingle on my mouth. Then suddenly they harden like nail heads. "Watch out!" she warns. And bam! There's a jarring crash. Lucia's face detonates, spraying beads of water in all directions, bolting me upright out of the dream.

At first I didn't know where I was. I looked around, lost, blinking my eyes to focus. The moon had moved to the far end of the upper windows. All was quiet at the farmhouse. The party over.

"Watch out!" Lucia's words still beat in my ears.

Watch out for what?

The barn door banged. I got up and leaned over the rail. It was Ray, stumbling in.

"Ray," I called out. "Hey man, what's up?"

"The assholes canned me, that's what!"

He was drunk. He took a couple shaky steps and

tottered to his knees on the plank floor. The open bottle in his hand splashed all over his shirt.

"They lie right to your face, the motherfuckers. Now they're making their move."

"Who? Who are you talking about?" I said, heading down the stairs. "Wasn't Caspian saying how glad he was you were sticking around?"

"Ha! That old man's a goner. They're stealing it out from under his dead nose. And I knew it. I psyched it. Just not like this. Not this fast. So fuck me."

He reached up, grabbed my vest and yanked me down to an inch from his sloppy mouth.

"Listen up. These people got to be stopped. You with me here, bellmaker?"

"You're drunk, man," I said, freeing myself from his grip.

He bounced a sideways look at the bottle in his hands. Then tossed it aside.

"This ain't drunk. This is primal rage."

"Whatever. Let's get you to your trailer."

"No. Can't go there. Not now. Help me up. I gotta show you something."

"Show me what?" I propped him up against the lathe.

"Shh! Keep your voice down." He pointed at the ceiling. "Kill the light. And close that god damn door."

After shutting the barn door and flipping the wall switch, I returned to find him talking to himself in the moonlight.

"Right, right," he muttered. Then he teetered his bleary-eyed way over to the stairs using band saws and worktables as crutches.

"Come here," he said in a forced whisper. "Hey, I said come here."

He had me pull out the bottom step of the stairs and reach into the hollow.

My fingers bumped against something.

A fat leather pouch.

"Unzip it," he ordered.

The pouch was stuffed with brass keys, silver keys, and plastic card keys all strung on a carabineer.

"Crown jewels." He smiled. "Gitcha into everywhere. Or just about."

I flipped the keys over in my hand. I didn't know what to make of them.

"Okay, okay, put'em back," he said.

After I zipped it up, he slapped the pouch from my hand and dropped it back into the cavity under the bottom stair.

"Whatever you do, man, don't let 'em find that on you. Now put the tread back."

I pushed the wooden step back into place.

"And you're showing me this because…?"

The crunch of golf cart wheels passed the barn and faded off. Ray mumbled something to himself. Then he asked me to help him onto the forklift.

"They think they're done with me? I got some bad news for them. I've worked too hard to be bled to nothing. I go gather me up a posse comitatus and come down on their heads like a shit avalanche."

Ray's words slurred in my ears as I gave him a boost onto the seat of the forklift.

He struggled to pull the pack of cigarettes from his shirt pocket.

"Now, git outta here. You don't want to be seen with me. Guilt by association and all that."

"Fine." I started for the stairs.

"Whoa." He called me back. "One last thing."

This is crazy. Taking orders from a drunk.

"The code," he said.

"What code?"

"The god damn key pad that's what."

"What key pad?" I said.

"Death's Door, where else?"

"Hey man, I just got here."

"Shhh…okay, okay, sorry," he said. "My brain is sawdust."

He worked a cigarette to his mouth, bit off the filter and spat it out.

"Now listen. Are you listening?" He struck a match on the dashboard. "Lock this into your head like it's your lover's phone number, and never, never tell nobody. If they find out, poof! People disappear around here. So don't even write it down."

He lit the cigarette, sucked in the smoke and blew it in my face.

"Code's probably only good for a couple days, anyway. They'll recode after JT leaves. You ready?"

He slowly whispered a string of twelve numbers, which he repeated over and over. Then had me repeat it back to him.

"1-2-7-2-7-7-1-2-1-2-1-7."

"You got it," he said, and leaned back against the

seat.

"They gave you this code?"

"God no. Only JT, Roe, and Gudrun know the code. But I got my ways. Survival insurance. Like gold in the bank."

"And what am I to do with it?"

"Just in case." He pointed the cigarette at me. "Hey, I don't trust just anyone, y'know."

"Yeah… meaning?"

"What I'm gonna tell you."

Footsteps scuffled along the gravel road. Someone was out there. More than one.

The barn door creaked.

Ray flung his cigarette at the door.

"Shit!"

He fired up the forklift and floored it.

"Come and get me you pussy-ass motherfuckers!"

The bell lurched and swayed from the forks. The machine's headlights burst on three startled faces. All men. I recognized the rhinoceros, or Gorno, as he's called.

The men easily dodged the oncoming rig. One guy jumped up onto it and tackled Ray to the floor. The forklift idly rolled to a stop. The others huddled over him, their flashlights in his face, blinding his eyes.

"Just hand them over and we'll be on our merry way," one said.

Ray shaded his eyes with a flat hand. "Gave'em to Julian."

"Julian sent us, man," one said.

"Gave it to Roe, then."

"Bullshit!" Gorno barked.

"Where are they, dickhead?!" another guy demanded.

"Right here," Ray bit down on the heel of his left hand and threw a punch with his right, knocking the guy back on his heels.

Gorno grabbed Ray by the neck, snatched him up off the floor as easy as a bag of rags, and heaved his body against the row of lockers. The other two joined in and started pummeling him mercilessly.

The impulse to jump in and help Ray was hard to contain. But it was not my fight. Instead, I unsheathed one of the tuning forks on the worktable and pitched it past their heads striking the bell dead on.

BWANGGG!

The men jumped. Their heads jerked and twisted every which way. The peal even stunned me.

Flashlight beams slashed the air and finally froze on the bell that rocked from the forks right behind their heads.

Gorno grabbed the base of the bell with one hand, trying to snuff out the sound. But the bell's lasting vibration still jangled the metal tools and equipment in the shop.

"Did you hit that thing?"

"Hell no!" one of the men said.

"Idiot!" Gorno hollered.

"I didn't do it!"

The barn door creaked.

"Okay, get him outta here," Gorno ordered.

"He's not there."

"What?"

"Ray's gone!"

Gorno swung his flashlight beam around the floor. "Well god dammit, go get him!"

The men scrambled outside.

"And when you got him, bring'em to me at his trailer!"

Gorno's flashlight searched the shop. He panned a slow stripe of light across the power equipment. His hulking shape lurched in my direction and with it came that medicinal smell again. A stinging antiseptic odor.

I stood motionless, heart racing.

The brute's got nothing on me. Not that he couldn't make something up.

As he drew closer and closer, I looked around for some tool to defend myself. It was either that, try to run, or get squashed like a bug.

His flashlight beam swiped across my torso. I was a split second from bolting when something flickered in the barn door. Another one of those flame-blue feather things. My flesh puckered with goose bumps.

Gorno sensed something too. He pivoted around and pointed his flashlight at the door. By then the thing had vanished and taken Gorno's attention with it. He started for the door and tunk! His foot kicked Ray's bottle. When he shone a light on it he saw something else and plucked my tuning fork off the floor. He held it up and examined the odd looking thing with his flashlight.

Come on big guy, I mentally urged. *Just leave, and leave my tuning fork here.*

A boom sounded outside like the backfire of an engine, followed by a thunderous roar. Gorno dropped the fork on the table saw with a clink, and split.

The wheels of a cart tooled away up the road. The barn fell silent, leaving only the ting of tuning forks throbbing in their jackets. I set my hand on the forks to quiet them and waited, listening in the dark for a couple minutes. Then I eased the barn door shut, climbed the wooden stairs, and flopped my body down on the cot. I lay there unable to sleep, synapses firing in my brain.

What was all that about?

I tried to figure out Ray's intentions. The drunk never got around to telling me why he gave me the pass code to Death's Door and the hiding place of his confiscated keys. Seemed like privileged information to hand over to a total stranger.

Maybe he knew his days were numbered and needed to free himself of it. Pass it on to the nearest person he felt he could trust.

In retrospect, if Ray hadn't shown me the keys and made me memorize that pass code, things would not have played out the way they did.

Outside, an owl hooted, "Wha-wha-wha-whoo, whoo-hoo." A couple seconds later another owl, far off, hooted back, "Wha-wha-wha-whoo, whoo-hoo."

After a fitful sleep I woke up with the revelation that the columns and the beam needed to fortify the front entry would alter the look of the house. The facade would no longer be an exact representation of

Sylvia's crayon drawing. Seemed like a problem to me. It would make more sense to build a standing armature for the bell and install it in the front garden or wherever.

Outside the barn the early morning air felt crisp. Overnight the weather had changed. A breeze sifted through the upper branches. Autumn comes early in Wisconsin.

From the farmhouse came a gurgling of voices. As I walked about stretching my legs and inhaling the fresh scent of pines, I spotted a golf cart tipped against the side wall of the barn like a kid's abandoned toy.

So that's the crash I heard. Ray's drunken driving.

A crunch of wheels drew my attention to the road where two men came shuttling down the hill, their cart loaded with luggage. Day of departure for the workers.

My morning plan was to check in with Tandre, tell him about the front entry dilemma and see if he wanted the bell re-located. Then I would hike to the top of the hill and determine the prime tone of the land to tune the bell. But first I needed food. Reaching into the pockets of my shop coat, I dug out the leftovers I'd wrapped up from the banquet. Back inside the barn, I set it all on a worktable.

Seeing the food laid out reminded me of the times Lucia and I would eat at her sewing table in my studio amidst a jumble of materials she'd gathered from here and there. She had parrot feathers, ostrich and rooster feathers, swatches and scissor cuttings of woven and metallic cloth, sand dollars, sea urchin shells, and bone-white sticks of driftwood beaten smooth by the tides she combed off the beaches of San Gregorio and Pt. Reyes.

Gorging away at the leftovers I'd scrounged, I felt something rub against the back of my leg.

A scrawny gray cat purred at my feet.

"Hey there."

The cat meowed with a feeble cry. It brushed its cobwebbed whiskers against my jeans. Its fur ragged and dusty. Its tail was corkscrewed at the tip like it had been kinked in a door or caught in a trap. I peeled some morsels of meat from the ribs, set them on a napkin and fed the cat on the floor. After eating, the cat jumped up on the table and contentedly licked its paws and swabbed its chops. Little did I know at the time this cat would play a pivotal role in my future pursuits at the house.

The ATV keys hung on a hook by the loading dock door. I backed the trailer into the barn and positioned it under the bell. I was about to lower the bell onto the cart when I spotted a scrunched white envelope on the forklift seat. It had a little label with the name 'Ray Freely' printed on it. Inside were three slips of paper-- a paycheck for $3,125 dollars, a note of thanks from 'The Sylvia House,' along with details of departure time, luggage pickup, transportation to the airport, and a heavily worded warning in bold type reminding the now ex-employee of the legal fallout should he or she ever speak a word about the place, the project, and the people involved both living and dead.

It reminded me of the papers I was to sign which I

assumed were on Jean Tandre's oak desk where Julian dropped them.

Legally, I was still free to tell anybody about the place. Not that they'd believe a word.

Stuffing everything back in the envelope, I wondered if it was the keys those thugs were after or some other survival insurance Ray had tucked away. Seemed to me he'd return for his check, if and when he could. So, I anchored the envelope down on the worktable with a framing square. Then I slipped the roll of tuning forks into my backpack and headed out to talk to Jean Tandre.

The windows of the silo were dark, but seeing his golf cart parked out front, I went ahead and knocked. The arched door gave way. Curious, I went inside.

Before me was a sitting room with a round coffee table in the center surrounded by overstuffed chairs.

"Anybody home?"

No one answered.

"Jean Tandre?"

Behind the front door was a spiral staircase. I craned my neck and called up, "It's me, Joe Gandy... you up there?"

The stairs led to a small, fully equipped kitchen and dining nook with floor to ceiling cabinets neatly scribed to fit tight around the curved brick walls. Up another level I came to Tandre's bedroom. A huge ultra king bed hogged the space. His blue workman clothes folded on a chair, but no sign of him.

Then I heard a tapping sound above me.

"Hello?"

The top floor was furnished like a cozy architect's study with a drafting table surrounded by file cabinets and cubbyholes of blueprints. The tapping I'd heard came from a bumblebee banging its body against the sliding glass door that led outside to the balcony.

Walking to the door, I saw a crinkled piece of velum sticking out of a cabinet drawer. A bit of disorder in an otherwise clean and tidy space. I spotted another blueprint peering from a tube that had rolled against the foot of a cabinet. Tandre's Porch plans crossed my mind and I remembered the lights I'd seen blinking through these silo windows in the night.

Flashlight beams. Someone was up here rifling around and left without putting things away.

I opened the patio door and let the bumble bee fly free. Seeing a pair of binoculars hanging on a bracket next to the door, I stepped out onto the iron grate of the balcony and looked around. From that vantage point most of the property and outlying areas were visible. Quite the lookout for Tandre to survey his domain.

Through the binoculars I could see in detail the backside of the house. It wasn't constructed all crazy like the front. The lap siding ran straight and the windows were plumb and spaced at uniform intervals. A delivery road descended to a lower level behind the house and dead-ended at the domes of the Greenhouse and the Porch. There was a truck and semi-trailer backed up to one of the two loading docks. A sign on the side of the trailer read: ALL WAYS MOVING. A man was working on the dock, erecting some sort of screening material around it. Across the driveway from the dock a tractor sat parked next to a catchall yard of construction materials and stacks of iron scaffolding.

I circled the deck of Tandre's silo and turned the binoculars onto the farmhouse where I saw folks gathered on the porch. Gudrun's blonde bob of hair stood out among them and I could hear Sylvia's chickadee giggle.

Out on the road in front of the farmhouse security guards dug through the luggage. No doubt searching for things that the powers deemed forbidden-- no cameras, no photos, no diaries, no souvenirs.

Behind the farmhouse Ray's Airstream trailer sat on a large graded area. A number of electrical hookups stuck out of the ground where more trailers must have parked at one time. There was no sign of Ray or his motorcycle.

"Hey, you up there!" someone shouted.

Down on the ground near the base of the silo stood a man eyeballing me through the scope of a rifle.

"Its okay," I called down, dropping the binoculars to my waist.

"Don't you move!"

I could hear the stomp of his boots coming up the tower's iron stairs and shaking the balcony grate.

"Who the hell are you and what are you doing up here?"

The guy wore a deer hunter's vest and a camouflage bandana wrapped taut around his head. The hunting rifle hung from a strap over his shoulder, pointing at my torso. The first armed display I'd seen. But I didn't take it as a sign of threatening things to come. Just the roughneck antics of a frustrated macho man.

"Lower that, okay? I'm working on a project with Jean Tandre. Have you seen him?"

"No." He dipped the barrel of the rifle. "And I don't know you. But whoever you are, you're not to be up here. So, down you go."

He questioned me about what I was working on with the architect as we descended the staircase and stepped outside.

"Be sure to find me after your meeting or I'll hunt you down." He swaggered off to the farmhouse.

Am I in, am I out? What a circus, I thought as I hiked up the hill past the helipad. The morning sun was rising in the east, stretching its fingers across the land, filling in the valleys with light. The warmth of it on my face reminded me of the first time Lucia and I made love. It was all about the sunshine. I had been teaching her how to weld. We were outside in the open yard behind my studio. At one point she lifted her goggles and blinked in the sunlight. She described the rainbow colors dancing on her eyelashes as she squinted at me. And in a flash of spontaneous arousal our lips met. The rest is a beautiful blur. It all happened in slow motion. Unforced. Unhurried. The shedding of clothes lazy as falling leaves as we moved into the studio where we spooled together, our bare flesh melting like butter into each other's lives.

"Well," she said afterward. "Talk about welding."

More memories of Lucia followed. The time she took me to Luther Burbank's gardens in Santa Rosa to introduce me to the famous thornless rose bushes.

"You see," she said. "If roses can shed their thorns, then so can you." And all the zany headdresses and feathered art pieces she crafted that so delighted people. Especially the red felt hat she made for me with a little bell stitched to its pointed top that changed my art forever.

If it wasn't for Lucia I would never have broken through the resentful shell I'd worn like armor against the world.

At fourteen I'd become a defiant little son of a bitch. An extreme reaction to my father's disappearing act. Or so I believed. Maybe I came out of the womb spitting tacks. An absent father didn't help. He didn't know where to fit my angry ass into his stainless steel life. My mother was barely there for me as well. Too busy scheduling society page venues and outings in one hand while polishing cherry wood furniture with the other. Both of them victims of the looking-good disease. She stood steadfast behind my father like a potted plant, fully accepting her place of invisibility. I didn't. I acted out. I bit back at the world with flint-sharp fangs.

It came to a head when I was expelled from high school at sixteen for inciting a brawl that crippled Randy Benker, a notorious bully. True, I'd orchestrated it all— a calculated food fight in the cafeteria to inflame the bully into escalating it into an all-out, chair-slamming rampage. The inevitable had finally happened and the timing couldn't have been worse. My father had just landed his dream job on Wall Street the day of the brawl. It was like I'd emasculated him. His face frost-white. My mother seething in disgust.

What to do with their teenage hellion? "No problem," I told them. I stayed on in San Francisco to live with Grandpa Frank.

Now, with the distance of time, I view things differently. I see the parental terror my father felt. When you live behind a looking-good mask and don't have a clue who you really are, how do you know how to be a father? Fortunately Grandpa Frank had a keen sense of himself. He also knew I was becoming a one-man riot. He understood my raucous and reactive personality and took me in. Just one hitch— "You're going to read for your rent, a book a week, and I do the picking."

Might as well fit me for a straight jacket. I detested reading and Frank had piles of books on the plank floor of his loft. Leaning towers of hardbound and paperback books that served as end tables for coffee cups, reading glasses, needle-nosed pliers and whatnot.

"Let's have you start with this one." Frank handed me, *One Day in the Life of Ivan Denisovitch*. He had me read it out loud to him while he re-upholstered a sitting bench for some art gallery owner.

Frank's choice of books seemed predictable. Your standard high school classics: *Grapes of Wrath, Old Man and the Sea, Diary of Anne Frank* along with stories from Native Americans. Looking back, the books shared a common theme: the struggle against unyielding adversity. They also shoved in my face how easy I had it at home growing up. Fed, clothed, and sheltered. Was I grateful? Far from it.

Frank also encouraged me to express my emotions

in sculpture. Vent my wrath. Spent more time in his studio than anywhere else. Beating cold-rolled sheet iron into bat people. Welding railroad spikes into hideous Christmas tree ornaments. Everything I made stood out like thorns. I would not be invisible. The anger and hostility I felt became my notoriety as an artist. It seemed to give me potency. A false power short-lived. At some point contempt for the world reverts back to the source— contempt of self. At 22 I found myself burning to oblivion at bullet speed. And my excesses didn't exactly lead me to any palace of wisdom.

Enter Lucia, and I discovered missing puzzle pieces of myself. Feelings and insights I'd kept under wraps or starved away, subsisting only on thin cabbage soup. That is until Lucia gave them permission to come out and play.

"One minute for silly," she'd say, daring me to do something spontaneous to make her laugh. Not my style. But I'd take the dare, make faces, or conjure up some quirky dance while she covered her mouth with her hand, willing herself not to crack up. After a few of these improvised episodes, I started thinking up outrageous antics for the next occasion. Little by little she found a way to unravel my humor and my hurt like a nest of tangled twine.

And did I ever really thank her?

Looking down across the September valleys and fields of Wisconsin, I had the driving desire to do just that. To get back into Tandre's Porch and call out Lucia's name. Bell or no bell, I'd find a way.

When I reached the top of the hill I hunkered down in the bent blades of grass. I unrolled the sheath of tuning forks as a wave of grief swelled up. I didn't resist. I let it swallow me. My whole life I never cried. But since Lucia's death, tears ran without a shutoff valve. Deep grief, once you catch it, there's no immunization. I wiped off the tuning fork with my coat cuff and pushed the fork's handle into the earth. Then I set one hand palm-down on the ground next to the fork and began my toning detection routine.

There are several ways to decipher the prime tone of the land. If you're a shaman or intuitive you might be able to sense it through your feet or the surface tension of your palms. My primitive method worked for me. It's based partly on the duration of time the tuning fork sustains the sound and the tonal vibrations I sensed in my inner ear.

With a conductor's baton I struck the tuning fork firmly, yet not hard enough to shift it from its footing. I shut my eyes and centered my attention on my inner ears, the tympanic cavity, listening to the quality and length of tone. A harmonic sensation, hard to describe in words.

Reaching for another tuning fork to cross-compare, I heard someone calling, "Dingo!"

The ground trembled with oncoming feet. Soon Sylvia and Gudrun were upon me. Their shadows blackened the grass.

"He makes bells," Sylvia told Gudrun.

"He does, does he."

"And he made one for me. Didn't you."

Sylvia wore a green corduroy jacket, long skirt, high boots, and a brown hat with a wide brim. The outfit made her seem older than her seven years.

"Don't move." She stepped right up next to me and pinched the skin on my neck. "There. Got it."

"Got what?"

"A tick."

She extended her hand an inch from my eyes to show me the wood tick she'd plucked from my neck. Then she squished the little black critter between her fingernails and flung it away.

"The state mascot," Gudrun joked. She took a tissue out of her fanny pack and wiped the tick juice from Sylvia's fingertips.

Gudrun introduced herself and asked me what I was doing. So I told them.

"I'm not following," Gudrun said. "You tune a bell to the sound of the land?"

"Every place carries its own signature tone," I explained. "It's what makes such a wide range of music around the world. All these different rhythms come straight out of the land and are expressed by the inhabitants. More to the point, we act out the vibe of the land where we live."

"I didn't know that."

"I didn't either until I started making bells."

Actually it was Lucia who heard about it from a traveling troupe of flute players. And I took it on seeing how significant the tone of the land is in bell tuning.

"Well, that explains my volcanic episodes," Gudrun said.

"Listen," I said, bouncing a tuning fork off my knee and holding it up to Sylvia's ear. "Do you hear that?"

"Ummm," she vocalized the sound, wiggling her body all around. "Gimme one?"

I handed her a fork.

"Just tap the tines against the edge of your hand or your knee."

Sylvia whapped the fork against her knee and lifted it up to her ear.

"Ninggg."

She hit it again and stepped up on her tiptoes for Gudrun to hear.

"Yes, I hear it sweetheart. So, why does a bell need to be in tune with the land?" Gudrun asked.

"To blend in. So the land and the life forms on the land, like the trees, the birds and the animals will accept it easily, in harmony, without resistance."

"Oh, I like that."

Gudrun got it.

"You want to try it?" I slid the low "C" tuning fork out of its sleeve. A hunch this land carried the root tone. I told Sylvia and Gudrun to hunker down in the grass next to the fork and listen close.

"Ready? Close your eyes and feel the tone." I tapped the fork. The sound held for a long time.

"Hear that? Hear how long it lasts? This could be the one. Either low C or high C."

"The one?"

"The key for the bell I brought for the house," I said.

"Where is it?" the girl asked.

"In the barn."

"I want to ring it."

"Sylvia, no." Gudrun shook a finger.

"Fine by me," I said.

"Don't let the cherubic disguise fool you. She's a troublemaker."

In the distance came the drone of an engine. We watched a plume of dust billow along the southern fence line and mushroom as the car stuttered to a stop. A figure stepped out and opened a gate.

"It's either Jean or Ray," Gudrun said. "They're the only ones with access to that gate."

"Ray has a motorcycle," Sylvia said.

As the car approached, I noticed Tandre driving and someone in the passenger seat. Seeing us, he slowed down and brought the Jeep to a halt.

"Jean!" Sylvia ran to him shaking a tuning fork in the air.

Tandre pulled himself out of the driver's seat looking disheveled.

"Bonjour, mon ami. What are you doing up here?"

"We came up to say goodbye to everybody and now we're looking for Dingo. Have you seen him?" She didn't wait for an answer. She rapped the tuning fork against her knee and held it up to his ear. "Hear that? You must come with us. We're going to the barn to ring bells." Sylvia peered into the car at the hooded passenger. "Who's that with you?"

"Questions and more questions."

"Watch out, she's a little cranky. Didn't get much sleep last night," Gudrun said. "You?"

Tandre gave Gudrun a worried smile and then

turned to me. "I have some things to take care of but I haven't forgotten Charles' request to hear your bell. We'll need to bring it down to the house and through the tunnel. Can you manage that?"

"I built a scaffold and found a furniture dolly."

"Tres bien. I'll call Ray. We'll need him, too."

He either didn't know what happened, or Ray was okay and around somewhere.

Gudrun must have picked up an unspoken signal in Tandre's face. She turned to Sylvia and me.

"You guys go ahead. I'll come by the barn in a little while."

"Dingo!" Sylvia called out for her lost dog as we headed to the workshop.

No dog came.

Walking past the now empty farmhouse the scraggly cat I'd fed earlier dashed out in front of us.

"That's Barney the barn cat," Sylvia said. "We're not supposed to feed him so he'll catch mice."

Sylvia pulled open the barn door.

"Where's Ray?" she asked.

"Don't know."

"Everybody's leaving." She looked up at me for a response.

None came.

"Are you staying around?" she asked. Her eyes vacant of that Sylvia sparkle.

"Just here to tune and install the bell." I pointed to it hanging from the forklift.

"Ha," she half-chuckled. "It's funny looking."

I explained how the front entry of the house was not built strong enough to carry the weight of the bell. It would need columns to bear the load and they'd make the house look different than her crayon drawing.

Sylvia said she'd think about it and talk to her Dad. Then she confessed that she never really liked the front of the house.

"Daddy's idea. He wanted something fun and not foonernal.

"Funereal?"

"Yeah, whatever that means."

"He probably meant not cold and gloomy-looking."

"He asked me to draw him a picture," she said.

"So that's how it happened."

"You said I could ring the bell."

"Let's get you up on the trailer." I leaned over to lift her up but she batted me away and climbed up by herself.

"Bells have a long history going way back to ancient China," I said, fetching the mallet. "The Chinese people believed bells had special powers."

Sylvia gave me a quizzical look.

"What powers?"

"Uh…" I paused, wondering how to explain it to a seven-year old. "Well, they thought the sound of a bell could cure illness. That it could help women with child birth, and protect goats and sheep from predators like wolves."

"Can it bring a dead body back to life?"

"Not that I know of."

"Can it help souls pass on to their rightful place on

the other side without getting stuck in between?"

I should have known who I was dealing with.

"Can it tell me everything I need to know so I don't have to go to school?"

"That, no, but if you ring it, maybe your dog will hear it and come home."

"Dingo, yes! I want my Dingo back."

I offered her the mallet.

"Can you handle this?"

She wrenched it out of my hand. But wielding it took some doing. Her first strike hit nothing but air.

"Try again."

She chopped at the bell like a hatchet, clipping the ridge along the bottom.

DTHONG!

She dropped the mallet. "I kinda did it."

"Let me help you." I picked up the mallet and set it on her shoulder. "Swing it like a baseball bat. Choke up on the handle and go for the fences. You ready?"

"Ready."

"Aim for this place right here."

Pointing to the sweet spot, I noticed a yellow streak above it— the nick in the metal where the tuning fork struck it.

"Sorry," I whispered and rubbed my finger along the bright scar.

"What's that?" Sylvia said.

"Nothing. Now widen your stance. Bend your knees a little bit."

She didn't wait for me to get out of the way. She took a big breath, reared back and whammed the bell with all she had.

BWONGGG!

Sylvia's hat blew off. Her startled eyes doubled in size as the sound detonated. She covered her ears with her hands. The mallet flopped off the trailer onto the barn floor.

"Wooo!" She whooped and hopped around, jiggling her hands in the air like tambourines as the toll played on.

Outside the barn Gudrun appeared, speaking to the rifleman who'd confronted me on the silo balcony. Gudrun's clenched face and finger pointing suggested a heated exchange. But their words were muted by the tones still reverberating off the bell.

After the man left, Sylvia jumped down off the trailer and dashed to Gudrun.

"I rang the bell. Did you hear it?"

"Yes. What a wonderful sound," Gudrun said with subdued excitement. She took the girl's hand and walked into the barn. "Jean says he'll meet you at the north door of the house with your bell and things. Do you know where that is?"

"I do. And say, I wonder if you could do me a big favor?"

"I'm going to ring it again!" Sylvia scooped the mallet up off the floor.

"No." Gudrun was firm. "We have to go."

Then, sensing something, Gudrun wheeled around on the balls of her feet. Outside the barn a feathery blue flame quivered in the air.

"Just one more." Sylvia climbed back up onto the

trailer.

Gudrun advanced with slow, soft steps toward the radiant light.

"There it is again." I squirmed, chills jangling my spine.

"You see it?"

"Yes."

"Not everyone sees them," she said.

"What are they?"

"Nansa. A type of light being. They started showing up a couple months ago."

Nansa, I said the name to myself.

Gudrun lifted her right palm as a greeting of peace. Slowly the aqua-blue feather drifted into the barn and hovered there, brilliant as the fire cone of an acetylene torch.

"Ahh," Gudrun sighed.

"What do they do?" I muttered.

"Charles described them as knitters whose work is to help mend the rays of union that once joined the physical and spirit worlds."

Knitters.

Hearing that, my body settled and I gazed at the Nansa with welcome eyes.

It's difficult to describe the feeling you get seeing these specters if you've never been in their presence. Words like 'magical' and 'other-worldly' don't cut it. Just seeing them shakes up all your pre-conceived notions of what constitutes the real world. You can no longer deny there are spiritual beings afoot. All you can do is gape in awe.

BWONGGG!

The bell bong alarmed us. Gudrun's body bristled. We both whirled around and saw the culprit, Sylvia, holding her ears and laughing herself silly at having surprised us.

When we turned back, the Nansa had gone.

Gudrun shook a finger at Sylvia. "Prankster."

"Yessss." Sylvia chuckled.

"Didn't you see the Nansa?"

"Where?"

"You missed it."

The bell tone faded away.

"That's the longest I've seen a Nansa remain in one place," Gudrun said. "Usually they flit here and there out the corner of your eye."

Something pinged repeatedly. Gudrun yanked a satellite phone from the pocket of her canvas coat, excused herself and walked off.

Up until then I hadn't realized Gudrun's earthy beauty. A sturdy, big-boned body with a moon face, cheeks smooth as sand dunes, and deep-set eyes. Could be 35, could be 45. A big sister maturity in camping clothes. She carried herself with a survivor's self-reliance that spoke of hard, simple work. The bread baking and firewood of remote lands.

I lowered the bell onto the trailer and had the girl help me gather and load up the materials for the scaffold. Gudrun returned looking distant and grim.

"What happened?" Sylvia asked her.

"Nothing, sweetie." Gudrun forced a half-smile,

then turned to me. "I'm sorry, you were asking me for a favor?"

"I need some help. I was wondering if you'd be willing to drive the ATV and trailer down to the house while I bring the forklift."

"I guess I can do that."

"Thanks," I said. "I'd ask Ray, but I don't know where he is. Do you?"

"I've driven the ATV before." Gudrun deflected my question.

Something was up. I could sense it. Gudrun knew something about Ray she wasn't telling.

Sylvia pelted Gudrun with questions about the hooded woman who was in the car with Jean Tandre. Gudrun told her the woman lived in Newgrange and that her eight-year-old daughter was missing.

"Jean is going to take the woman inside to see if her daughter has gone away."

"Can I come?"

"Not this time, sweetheart."

"Why? Why can't I go?"

"Because we need to get you ready for our little adventure."

"What adventure?" Sylvia's eyes swelled.

"Our secret adventure," Gudrun whispered.

"What's that?"

"I can't tell you. It wouldn't be a secret then."

After loading the trailer, Gudrun followed me down the hill in the ATV. Tandre's golf cart was parked at the north door of the house. The hooded woman sat slumped next to him in the seat. Gudrun tossed me the keys to the ATV and walked away with Sylvia still pestering her about their secret adventure.

"The bell will have to wait," Tandre said. "Would you help me here? I can't locate Ray."

It wasn't the time to tell him what I knew about Ray. I helped the distraught woman out of JT's cart. She could barely walk upright. Tandre unlocked the door. The woman sobbed and tightly gripped my hand as we went into the house.

Inside I heard rumblings and distant voices echoing off the walls. Tandre looked unfazed by them. He pushed ahead of us, unlocking a door off the corridor I hadn't seen before.

We entered a breezeway to the Greenhouse. Shafts of sunlight winked through the towering layers of leaves that spread in a multitude of fan and feather shapes. The humid air was alive with the fluted songs and haunting cries of unseen birds. We crossed the arched bridge over a stream of water that funneled between boulders and pooled into a broad lagoon surrounded by staghorn ferns, orchids and clusters of exotic flowers I didn't have names for.

The path ended at the limestone clearing across from Death's Door. Tandre punched the code on the security keypad. I didn't think to check if he was using the same 12-digit code Ray had me memorize.

Once inside the mudroom, I helped the woman off with her hooded coat and shoes. Her long brown hair a tangled, worried mess. Her young face looked gray and haggard with don't-look-at-me eyes.

We crawled through the tunnel and stepped up the ramp onto the deck of the Porch in silence. Tandre spoke gently to the woman as he stood beside her at the podium.

"Katherine Magnuson," she breathlessly called her missing daughter's name.

"A little louder," Tandre said.

"Katherine Magnuson."

I hugged the back wall hoping the child's face would not appear. That she was safe somewhere. A friend's house. Anything.

The mist stirred. A child's face formed. Her shining eyes peeled open.

"Mama!"

"No! Please God, no." The woman wilted, holding her chest as if her heart had caved in.

Tandre reacted instantly, bracing her limp body.

"I see you, Mama," spoke the sweet voice of the girl.

Tandre whispered something in the woman's ear.

She leaned forward at the podium, stifled her sobs, and after a few short, biting breaths said, "I see you too, Katie. I see you too."

Two feathery lights appeared like sentries on each side of the child's face.

Nansa.

"I'm..." The child began to say something but her voice became warbled.

"Ask her to repeat what she just said." Tandre coached the woman.

"What did you say, Katie?"

"I'm sorry, Mama. I'm sorry I went to the river. I

know I'm not supposed to."

The woman swiped at tears running down her cheeks.

"Its okay, Katie."

"You're not mad?"

"No, no, I'm not mad."

"Oh, good," the child sighed. "I thought you would be mad at me and Toby 'cause we… "

Again the child's voice distorted.

"Could you say that again?"

"I miss you, Mama."

"Oh, I miss you so much," the woman sputtered and broke down, gulping breath.

"I'm not going to be coming home soon."

"Ahh, God." The woman's chin pitched back.

Again Tandre whispered an instruction.

"I know, I know," the woman said, shaking her head, unwilling to accept her daughter's death.

"Don't cry Mama. I got scared, but I'm better now. I have new friends. And you can come visit me."

Hearing that, hot tears welled up in my eyes. I rubbed at them with my fist and looked over at Tandre who stood behind the grief-wracked woman beaming with joy, loving every heart-wrenching second of it.

That's just strange. What's with this man?

"Where, Katie?" Tandre had the woman ask. "Where in the river did you go with Toby?"

"… playing hide and seek and…" The child spoke but again her voice crackled.

"Where, Katie?"

"… climbed out on the willow tree."

"By the sandy beach?"

"I fell..." The child's voice broke up again.

Tandre stepped next to the woman and shifted his weight at the podium. It didn't help. There was too much distortion to hear the girl's voice clearly.

"We're still learning how to play the instrument," Tandre explained.

Out the corner of my eye I noticed Gudrun standing alone on the ramp. When I looked back the child's face was dissolving into the misty cloud.

Gudrun padded past me in her socks. She began to help the woman away from the podium. The woman took a couple wobbly steps then whirled around at Tandre, wild-eyed and rageful.

"No!" she shouted. "Not my Katie!"

Tandre enclosed her in his arms and rested his head on her shoulder. For a while she merely whimpered there. Then all of a sudden she broke out of his arms.

"I was with you!" she hissed, and pushed Tandre away. "You!"

Tandre swallowed her again in his arms. She wrestled in his embrace like a weary boxer.

"Damn you!" The woman's words were muffled by Tandre's shoulder.

Gudrun gently freed the woman from Tandre's hug and ushered her off the deck. When the two reached the mouth of the tunnel, another shockwave struck the woman. Her body contorted and she wailed. "I want her back! I want my Katie back!"

Gudrun comforted her.

Tandre and I watched them crouch and depart on

all fours, their silhouettes disappearing into the tunnel like two lumbering animals.

The ordeal left me depleted. Hearing the child say she was okay after drowning in the river gave little relief. The mother's loss only triggered my own and a re-run of Lucia's death played out in my mind. Her loving face the morning she drove away. The fog-blind road. Her Dodge van rammed by a U-haul truck on the drivers' door and sent skidding sideways, upturned and tumbling over the guardrail and down that gorge. Her body whipped about like a rag doll in a clothes dryer until finally the vehicle stuttered to a standstill in the creek bed upside down, tires spinning to a dead stop.

I had hiked down that steep slope the next day, past hubcaps, pebbled glass, beer cans and trash to the dry creek where the van ended up. I stood there inflamed, helpless, unable to undo what was done, cursing God.

"Gandy, thanks for that." Tandre tugged me back to present time. "Come on now." He motioned me to follow him. "Let's go to the pit."

"The pit?"

"The orchestra pit."

Partway down the ramp Tandre veered to his right to a steep set of stairs.

"Watch your step," he said.

My feet edged their way in the darkness down the stairs until it leveled off at a flat, semi-circular area, which I took to be the orchestra pit.

Tandre moved to a wall under the ramp where he

pulled a little T-shaped socket wrench from his pocket. He slotted it in a recessed hole and rotated the shaft counter-clockwise. It disengaged an internal locking device. He gripped a hand pull and slid back a wide section of the wall.

A hidden passageway.

"In here," he said, and slipped the wrench back in his pocket.

He directed me down another ramp that sloped in a long 'S' curve deep into the bowels under the porch floor.

"You don't have any metal plates in your head do you?"

"And if I did?"

He disappeared into the darkness below. I heard a grappling sound. A light burst on. It came from a round miner's lamp strapped to his forehead.

"Grab a couple spots." He aimed the beam of his headlamp to a shelf ten feet from where I stood. "The big ones," he added.

After taking two handheld spotlights off the shelf, I turned one on. It lit up a hard black floor, rough like slate. I swept the light around the immense space. The ceiling was at least thirty-feet high. Concrete pilings the girth of Sequoia trees supported the floor above.

For a moment I lost the man. Then I heard a rattle sound and saw him rolling a wooden chest of tools across the floor.

"Over here!" His voice bellowed throughout the subterranean expanse.

He was moving toward a place where the ceiling

dipped low in the bowl-shaped center.

"The inner sanctum?" I asked.

"More like the pump house."

Tandre came to a stop between three sets of round magnetic discs the size of manhole covers. The edges of the discs were machined smooth and buffed bright.

"So, this is the source of the throbbing in my feet," I said.

"You've heard the saying, 'It's all done with mirrors.' Well here it's all done with magnets and some highly exacting geometric planes."

The air under the porch was dry and still, except for a faint background moan, barely audible, like a far off foghorn snoring away. Until then I didn't know magnetism emitted sound waves.

Tandre had me place the spotlights into brackets attached to two nearby posts. He pulled a large, hard acrylic wrench from the tool chest. Then he motioned me toward one of the magnets.

"Hold this while I tighten it."

Seizing the magnetic disc with both hands, I realized it was actually two plates with a narrow gap between them.

"Careful, don't get your face too close, it'll suck the fillings out of your mouth."

Leaning away, I could make out the profiles of more magnets positioned in wider and wider circles around me on higher stands.

Tandre saw me gawking around.

"It's a force field of magnetic torsion. The slightest shift or rotation can alter everything. Surely you of all people would understand. It must be similar to all the fussy mathematics and metallurgical equations that are involved in producing one of your bells."

Hearing Tandre talk about magnetic torsion aroused a spark of inspiration I hadn't felt since before Lucia's death— the idea of making magnetic bells.

"Okay, so much for Aton," he said.

"Aton? You have names for the magnets?"

He didn't respond.

Zt!

"There's that zapping sound," I said.

"Ah, you heard that? Of course, given your finely tuned ears."

"What is it?"

"There's a little leak in the mechanics. It's intrinsic to the friction of polarities that sustains the ultrasonic force field."

"And that means?"

"Some rather dubious ones trickle in."

"You're talking about ghosts."

"We prefer to call them 'Leakers'. Minor annoyances. They appear at times around the Porch as unattended shadows. Some are quiet. Then there are those that give off a disembodied wail or shriek."

"Like the scream of pain I heard up there on the ramp last night."

"A bit of static in the reception."

"You call that static?"

"Or you could call it a stray burst of pre-mortem fear and agony."

"Come again."

"What you heard was the terrified utterance of someone long passed in their final throes of a violent death."

"Oh my God," I gagged.

"Most people can't hear them. Those that do get quite a start."

"So, are these Leakers harmful or just spooky?"

"They're slow, rather dense. The Nansa take care of them. They police the borderland between worlds. Clear the way, so to speak. Keep out the riff-raff. You'll hear that sizzle sound when they catch them, much like those outdoor zappers that electrocute insects."

"And you can't seal them out?"

"Doing that would choke the portal and the transmission of souls would cease. It's a small price to pay."

"Sounds like dissonance," I said.

"Spoken like a bellmaker. A hint of dissonance is essential for communication to occur." Tandre lifted his right hand and pressed his thumb and index finger together. "But we're talking minute amounts here. Barely a trace. Infinitesimal. At this finer, heightened level of metaphysical energy anything more can drag the frequency levels and be highly destructive."

"How so?"

Tandre smiled devilishly.

"Allow me to give you a demonstration."

He opened the knurls on the wrench and applied it to the fitting in the center of the magnet.

"Go out and watch the cloud as I loosen the pins and widen the gap between these two plates."

Curious, I headed up the ramp to see Tandre's show and tell. I stood with my back against the wall of the orchestra pit. In no time the cloud turned a sickly, gooey gray. A pressure plugged my ears as the once misty egg drooped heavily from where it floated and warped into an oily knot. Flat, serpentine forms uncoiled from the knot and oozed out into space like pulls of black tar. Ear-piercing screeches stung my eardrums as the oily knot ruptured into a thousand twisted faces all gnashed together in a writhing foam.

"Alright!" I wailed, jogging back down the ramp waving my hands in the air. "I get it!"

"Sorry to crack open the sewer." Tandre chuckled. "Not a pretty sight. But you must admit it speaks louder than words. Things can deteriorate to a dangerous level if the magnetic plates are not properly tuned at a high vibratory rate."

Zt!

"Hear that?" he said.

Zt! Zt!

"That's the zapping of Leakers being munched by Nansa."

Looking up the ramp I saw little thunderbolts of electric-blue light.

Zt! Zt!

"We brewed up a little feeding frenzy for them," Tandre said.

"Leakers," I said under my breath.

"Good thing they don't know how to organize," Tandre went on. "Otherwise we'd have a pesky battle on our hands. Now, take hold of the magnetic plate again so we can fine-tune the instrument. Ray usually handles this."

That's when I shared about the men who came to the barn the previous night and beat Ray bloody.

"Ray's a hot head and a loud mouth," Tandre said. "Irritates everybody. He's been in more fights here than Muhammad Ali. Fired, rehired. They'll call him as soon as they can't find something or do something. He'll be back. He's a boomerang, he always comes back."

After we tightened down a couple more magnetic plates, Tandre wanted to test the audio reception on the Porch. As I trailed after him across the floor, I seized the moment.

"Can I call for someone?"

We stopped at the base of the ramp. I told him how my girlfriend had been recently killed in an accident on a mountain road.

Tandre's headlamp blazed in my eyes. "So, that's the grief I sensed from you when we first met in the lobby." He rolled the tool chest back to its place. "Tell me about her."

"A classic Mediterranean beauty," popped out of my mouth as we started climbing the ramp. "With a smile that would make an army drop its weapons. Not perfect. A bit high-strung and stubborn, but most of the time exuberant."

Tandre nodded, so I continued. It felt good to talk about Lucia.

"First time I met her was in my Grandpa Frank's studio. She'd come to get some upholstery tips from him. Then she came to an art exhibit. I had a couple pieces of sculpture. Angry stuff. One was a bust of a man with a fist for a face welded out of 16-penny nails. She made a comment about it. I forget. I thought it was shallow. But those days I thought everyone was shallow. Turns out she's a sculptor and multi-media artist. One day she brought a couple pieces to show my Grandpa. Hats with camel-faced pillow people quilted in a crazy collage of photo-printed fabrics. Whimsy with abandon. The other side of the moon from my work. She was with some actor at the time. Then she reappeared in my life a couple years later and that was that."

"That was...?"

"That was love and it terrified me. Opening my heart to someone, it was like being lost in a foreign country and not speak the language."

Tandre listened to me, totally absorbed. So I went on.

"Like so many things in life there's always a hitch. My grandpa thinks it's a law of the universe. Nature's way of injecting some agitation to keep us humans from becoming too complacent."

"Ho-ho!" Tandre hooted in agreement. "The hitch, yes, I know it well."

"The hitch in our case turned out to be her parents. Money driven. Elitist. Not unlike my own. Right off they didn't approve. Even though I'd changed my ways they saw me as a monster. The outlaw artist. Not for their daughter. They tried to intervene and keep her away from me. It backfired. Just heightened her attraction. Her father even hired a private detective to shadow me. Find some dirt. Seemed like an easy task given my reputation for trouble. But that backfired too when the detective and I became fast friends."

Tandre chuckled. I was sure he'd had a number of private detectives tail his ass.

"Before long she's living with me in my warehouse studio and my art changed from rebellion to bells."

"Go on," Tandre urged, pulling at his beard, his eyes fastened on me.

"We never spoke of marriage, and that was fine. Until one day something happened. I'd been away a few days installing a bell in a botanical garden when I realized what the commitment of marriage is all about. At least for me."

"And that is?"

"Only another person can open your heart. You can't do it alone. I didn't know that until I met her. Another hitch in the universe. But she wouldn't commit to marrying me unless I took a vow of non-violence. She knew my history of hostility. A short fuse and all the baggage that trails along with it."

"What is her name?" he asked, stepping out into the orchestra pit.

"Lucia."

"The name on the bell."

He remembered.

"Then came that morning three months ago," I continued. "A morning socked in with fog thick as fur. If you've ever been to San Francisco, you know what I mean. Lucia was going to give her parents the news about us getting married. Even though I hadn't made a vow of non-violence, she felt my thorns would drop off in time. I tried to stop her from going. Save her from being scorched by her parent's outrage. But like I said, she was stubborn. She insisted she do it face to face. So, she drove her van up Mt. Tamalpais and that's the last time I saw her alive."

"Lucia." Tandre smiled when he spoke the name.

There it was again. That beaming grin of his. I couldn't understand what he enjoyed about death and the heartbreak of losing the love of your life.

"I'd give up my fee to see her," I said.

Tandre bowed gracefully and waved his free hand toward the stairs.

"Come then. Let's call your Lucia."

My body seized up as I stepped onto the deck of the Porch.

"What do I do?" I asked. "Where's the switch?

"The switch?"

"The mechanism that turns it on?"

"No switch. It works by where you stand. Don't tell anyone but the entire audio console is merely a prop with all your standard technical trappings to register audio levels. It has absolutely nothing to do with the transmission."

"All this is a prop?"

"Simply there to create the illusion of cutting edge electronics at work. You see, we live in a time where people believe more in plugged-in machines than the vibrational dynamics of stellated planes and the placement of fixed magnets. It's laughable."

Tandre reached down under the console, yanked an

electric cord out of a socket and bobbled the three-pronged plug in his hand.

"Everybody here is in a panic about Y2K. It's the cattle prod behind getting done as fast as impossible. Or so they infer. But this whole thing's made to look James Bond to comfort the guests. It's really no-tech. Simply where you stand and speak. The sweet spot. And you're standing on it."

"So, I can call her right here?"

"Simply face the mist."

I dipped my hand into my pocket and cradled the little bell Lucia had given me years before.

"Lucia Kazan," I called her name, waited a moment and called it again. "Lucia Kazan."

The cloud buffeted a bit. It was as if the sound of her name created an audible equation that pressed the motes into a new shape. Tiny tracer lights zinged out. The misty particles pulsed with prismatic colors and before my eyes a face melded into form.

"It's… it's Lucia."

I stood transfixed, like my dream, my heart banging against my chest. Only, when her face resolved, a calm of relief came over me. My shoulders drooped in sad surrender.

"Someone calls for me?"

"Lucia, it's me."

At first she didn't appear to recognize me. On impulse I pulled the little crotal bell out of my pocket and jingled it.

"It's me, Joe Gandy."

Lucia's face brightened. She was about to speak

when a scrubbing sound from the tunnel distracted me.

"Someone's coming," I told Tandre as a figure creeped out.

"What's going on here!" Roe struggled to his feet and frisked me with his eyes.

"We're tweaking the audio reception," Tandre said, walking to the rim of the deck.

I stepped back from the podium, and when I did, Lucia's face disintegrated into the mist.

"Unbelievable!" Roe was livid. "You sneak some woman from town in here. Who is she, another one of your sordid conquests?"

"Her little girl drowned in the river," Tandre said.

"So I hear." Roe strode up the ramp. "And people die every day. It's heartbreaking. But rules are rules. No mixing with the locals. We set the rules and we follow them. Except for you. No, you turn everything into your own pet entertainment."

"If you don't honor the locals then you're asking for severe reprisals. I know this from experience. And surely your rules allow for special exceptions."

"No, they do not. And your exception will make us the talk of Newgrange. Right now that woman is hysterical. She can't be consoled nor can she be trusted to keep her mouth shut. When the state and fire officials find out they'll shut us down! I've had it with you Jean!"

Seeing the vibrations of their squabbling shimmy the cloud, I realized how incredibly sensitive the acoustics of the Porch had been designed, registering every word, every breath.

This space is one enormous eardrum.

"You're tired, Leonard," Tandre said.

"Tired of you. This is your last day. The attorneys are drawing up a restraining order as we speak."

"Well then, that settled, and you're here, we can have that talk with Charles now."

"No! No more talk. The investors are on their way. I'm over my head with preparations for their tour."

"Then we better hurry. Gandy, why don't you bring in the bell. Leonard you need to hear this."

"Stop right there!" Roe roared at me. "There will be no bells. And don't say, 'But Leonard, this is not just any bell."

"This is not just any bell, Leonard," Tandre said.

"Of course it's not. It can't be just any doorbell. No, you have to go and commission some bizarre, new age enlightenment bell that costs a hundred thousand dollars. You can't simply go down to the Farm & Feed and buy some door chimes for ten bucks."

"Caspian specifically asked to hear Gandy's bell," Tandre said.

"I don't care what Caspian asked for."

"You're not answering to anyone these days, are you?"

"I said no. No budget, no bell. End of story."

Tandre smiled and motioned to me. "Ah, but the bellmaker is willing to waive his fee. Aren't you, Mr. Gandy?"

"The bell is yours. Free of charge," I said, moving down the ramp toward the tunnel. Which wasn't true since I'd already spent most of the down payment on debts.

"There, you see," Tandre said.

It felt like he was using me as bait to taunt the man. But Roe was not one to flinch or retreat.

"You don't know when to quit," Roe said. "No, you keep adding on until the foundation collapses under the weight of your endless demands. But all of that stops right here, right now. No more new things. You're finished, Jean. Finis."

"Is it really about the drawings, Leonard? About pocketing the patent?" Tandre gave Roe a toothy smile. "Or something else?"

Roe didn't give an answer. He simply stood there, stiff, seething through his nostrils.

"Okay then, you'll have your plans. Tonight."

Tandre was lying. Leading him on. I could tell by the flat, meatless tone in his voice that resounded in the tunnel as I kneeled at its mouth.

"Pack your bags," Roe said with cold finality. "I will not tolerate one more day of your reckless nature. This is far too precious."

"Ah yes, we must not humble the enterprise. If you build it they will come— the rich and famous that is. Right, Leonard? No public library here. No huddled masses for you. Can't have the small time, nobody deaths between lovers, or a forgotten soldier, or one's dear old mum. No power and prominence in that now is there? No, it's too precious. It must be by appointment only, ultra-exclusive, like a gilded country club. That's it Leonard, it's your Club Dead."

That started a sparring of words with both of them

barking at once.

As I pulled on my boots in the mudroom I felt like seizing the two by their ears and saying, 'Grow up, guys. You're sitting on a Mecca here. In no time there'll be pilgrimages to this house, busloads, bumper to bumper. So work it out.'

But here again, not my fight.

I went back outside to retrieve the bell wondering if Tandre and Roe would resolve their feud in my absence.

Working the forklift, I lowered the harmonic bell onto the furniture dolly. My heart felt lighter. Even though I'd only glimpsed Lucia for one sweet second, it was long enough to give me a lift and the prospect of seeing her even more.

While I waited for Tandre, a cart rolled up nearly pinning my legs against the trailer.

"What the hell are you still doing here?"

It was Julian at the wheel. A look of revulsion on his face.

"Back off," I said. "Caspian asked to hear the bell."

"The what?"

I pointed to the bell on the dolly by the door. "Don't they keep you in the loop?"

He looked over at it and scrunched up his nose. "No fuckin' way that's going in there," he said.

"Afraid so. And that's official."

"You have no say here," he said, shaking his head. "You're nobody. Squat."

The raw urge to beat the crap out of Julian swept through me like a gust of hot wind, but seeing the snarl and flared nostrils on his face I had a sudden revelation.

"Hey, I just figured out why I can't stand you."

"Good for you," he mumbled as he unclipped the walkie-talkie off his belt.

"You're the angry, arrogant asshole I used to be."

"Oh, ouch."

"An absent father, right?"

"Fuck you."

"I must be getting warm."

"Gorno, pick up," he blurted into the unit.

"Never got that loving touch, huh? So you cover up the pain with power."

"Hey, Gorno, I need you to drop whatever you're doing and get over to the north door. We got another straggler who needs sweeping up, over. The bellmaker dude, that's who, over. No, the guests are en route and I need to change my clothes and get ready to greet them, over and out."

As Julian spoke to Gorno, I spotted a hefty handgun strapped inside his jacket.

One serious firearm for an administrator's assistant.

A clunk sounded. Tandre emerged from the side door. He kicked a wedge under the door to hold it open.

"Just in time," I said.

"What now?"

"I'm being booted off the grounds."

"He's not on the short list," Julian explained.

"Screw your list. We have work to do," Tandre fired back.

"He's got ten minutes to be packed and gone."

"Not going to happen."

"Your name's not on the short list either." Julian grinned at the architect. "What do you make of that?"

"Pfff." Tandre blew out a breath of disgust between his lips. "Memento mori. No one gets out of life alive, Julian. And when you die you'll come face to face with the malignant scum you've chosen to become. What do you make of that?"

Julian slid the tip of his index finger across the bridge of his nose and pointed it at Tandre. "You look like you could use a good long nap, Jean. Heh-heh-heh."

"Go. Go interrogate somebody," Tandre fired back, waving Julian away.

Julian backed up the cart. "Ten minutes and counting." He smirked at me, then sped away.

Tandre caught the anger in my eyes.

"The man gets his thrills throwing rocks in the ponds of people's lives to see them splash. Don't waste your anger on him. That's how he owns you."

If only I had that point of view when I was a teenager.

We walked over to the dolly.

"You think it's going to fit through the tunnel?" I said.

Tandre eyed the bell for a moment, sizing it up against the tunnel dimensions in his mind.

"By a cat's whisker."

In hindsight, all the clues for what was about to happen bobbed in front of my nose in those last encounters. There was Tandre's eroding role as the Afterlife's creative director. There was Roe's noose-tightening control of the place. And now Julian's taunting words. Not just what he said, but the cocky vibe of malice and subversion. If I'd been observant I might have picked up on it. Could I have changed the course of coming events? Maybe. But my thoughts at that moment were focused on getting the bell inside and seeing my beloved.

Tandre helped me wheel the dolly down the corridor to the Greenhouse. He looked pale. Dispirited.

"You alright?" I asked.

"Families." He wagged his head and snorted air out his nostrils like a bull.

From that I construed he and Roe didn't kiss and make up.

Tandre turned to a panel next to the glass doors of the Greenhouse and shut off the misting system. As we rolled the dolly along the wet, mineral path, I remembered Julian protesting about the millions of dollars wasted on this jungle under glass.

"So, what's the purpose of the rain forest, if I may ask? I mean, it's breathtaking and beautiful, but it must have cost a fortune, and..."

"And?"

"Well, I'm sensing there's more to it than the theme park experience."

"There is, although Charles could never grasp it, while he was alive, anyway. Nor does Leonard to this day."

"Try me."

"Have you ever been to the Amazon?"

"Can't say I have."

"A rain forest is an ever-cycling fountain of creation. It's a continuous interplay of life and death, undivided and in virtual balance. You see, there is no actual death in a healthy rain forest. In their decomposition, the dead and dying vegetation donates to the life of the whole. It's one uninterrupted loop."

We rolled the dolly up to Death's Door.

"The Eden we lost," he added as he punched the code on the keypad.

I looked back at the deep green mass of leaves and vines.

"I get it. It's like the Porch," I said. "Where the spirits of the dead feed their knowledge to those living in the physical world."

"Yes, that's it. That's the united state."

We moved the harmonic bell into the mudroom and up to the mouth of the tunnel.

"Here goes," I said. "Moment of truth."

"It will fit." Tandre assured me.

His eyesight was dead on. The bell squeezed through by a hair.

As we hauled it out of the tunnel, a voice croaked over an intercom: "Jean Tandre, come to the lobby, you have a visitor."

He didn't acknowledge the summons. At least not noticeably. We heaved and tugged the bell up onto the deck floor. We were out of breath, and we weren't done yet. I went back for the scaffold timbers and hardware. By the time I returned, Tandre had a makeshift frame erected out of surplus aluminum magnet stands he pulled from under the floor. We jerry-rigged the bell an inch off the deck on a wobbly crossbeam.

"I call for Charles Caspian," Tandre boomed out, an agitation in his voice.

Caspian didn't come.

Tandre called his name again.

The cloud didn't budge.

Zt!

Tandre tried troubleshooting— standing at different places at the podium, leaning to one side, then another, altering the timbre of his voice.

Still, nothing happened.

Irritated, Tandre tamped his foot on the porch floor. He plucked at his beard and stared intently at the cloud for a minute before turning to the bell.

"Hand me your mallet."

He gripped the handle with both hands where it met the head, stepped up to the bell and gave it a light tap an inch above the rim.

DTHNNGGG

A kiss. That's all. Yet, in these acoustics, the toll filled the space with absolute clarity, bringing a purring sensation to my skin.

"Imagine how an orchestra would sound in here," he said. "And they won't even give me a bell." Tandre handed the mallet back to me. "Okay, let's see if we sprung the clam."

He stepped back to the podium and called out Caspian's name.

The cloud quivered and stopped. Then it began to swirl and gleam, sluggishly at first, as though unwilling to form Caspian's face.

Ultimately it gave way.

"Hello Jean," the old man's voice resounded off the walls.

"There you are, Charles. Thought you might not make it."

"Oh, how so?"

"I called several times. Nothing happened."

"I only just now felt the tug."

"Well, something must be blocking the way. We primed all the plates."

"Odd. I'll look into it on this end. Is Leonard with you?"

"No, Charles. Leonard and I are at each other's throats," Tandre said. "He wants the plans, which I'm willing to give in exchange for a service contract. The instrument will need tuning every now and again. Leonard thinks he can simply hire some maintenance man."

"This is not good, Jean. I know you two have been through a long, hard grind."

"Now he's ordering me off the premises."

After a pause, Caspian said, "Perhaps a little time away is best. Allow the dust to settle. Still, I need to speak with both of you."

"The man is becoming more rigid by the hour. But I'll persist," Tandre said.

"Do what you can."

"I did bring Mr. Gandy and his harmonic bell at your request."

"Ah, the bell, yes."

"Shall we?"

"Ring the bell by all means," Caspian said. "And may it bring some harmony back to the house."

"Not too hard," Tandre said, pressing his hands firmly on his end of the beam, holding it steady.

I gave the bell a gentle rap with the mallet right on the sweet spot.

BWOHHH-ONGGG

The peal stunned the space in a vibrant series of ascending tones. The sound waves poured through me like a warm river, releasing the tight-strung muscles in my neck and shoulders from my encounter with Julian.

Tandre and I turned to the cloud where kaleidoscopic pinwheels of light whirled around Caspian's face. Then the entire cloud brightened and expanded, fanning out in horizontal arcs like Saturn's rings, before retreating as the hum tone quieted.

"Oh my!" Caspian gushed. "Jean, can you hear me?"

"Yes, Charles."

"Could you see anything different?"

"Oh yes, a dramatic change in the brilliance and formation of the mist around you. Bands of multi-colored light spread from the cloud in rhythmic rings."

"The bridge is widening," Caspian said. "Sound it again. Please. Ring your bell once more."

"Give it all you got," Tandre said.

"Alright, hold tight." I pulled the mallet head back to arms length as I turned my torso at the hips and let fly.

BWOHHH-WOO-WAH-ONGGG!

Talk about a Big Bang. Immediately the cloud around

Caspian billowed with luminous waves blown outward in all directions at once. Then, aqua-blue Nansa unfurled as if they were being peeled away by hidden hands.

Tandre stepped to the podium, his arms outstretched and swaying like an orchestra conductor, his head lifting higher and higher, drawn to the star-like clusters that sprung around the top of the cloud like a crown of diadems.

"Again," Caspian urged, his face enveloped in light. "Ring the bell again."

Tandre rushed back to the bell grinning ear to ear. He leaned on the beam to keep it from shifting as I reeled back and hammered the bell with the mallet hard as I could.

BWOHHH-WOO-WAH-ONGGG!

I didn't wait for the tones to settle, I pounded it again.

BWOHNGG!

And again.

BWOHNGG!

This time the toll of the bell induced multiple harmonics that percolated around my ears like a thousand calliopes. When I turned around, the cloud had ballooned in size. Caspian's face was no longer visible. Laser-sharp jets erupted from the top of the cloud illuminating the cavernous, conch-like interior of the Porch.

Now I could see the space all lit up. A masterful construction only a giant could have fashioned. The Porch had been built like a polarized gyre. Huge mortise and tenon-jointed timbers wound upward in a torquing rotation to the apex of the dome where they triangulated into a multi-faceted star. Around floor level, the hewn wooden members curved downward in reverse and converged in a series of receding rings to a center point in the concave floor.

Tandre thrust a finger at the ceiling, his mouth blown open in amazement. He was pointing to a faceted lens of diamond-sharp light that looked to be slicing through a dimensional wall into the air of the space. Soon another lens appeared next to it, lightning bright. And with them, something else— a high, shimmering symphony of chimes that played off the changing bell tones only at a higher, livelier harmonic.

A deep thrumming vibration wobbled beneath me, revving like the engine room of a steam ship. It anchored my legs and feet to the floor of the deck as if the force of gravity had just quadrupled. I gazed down into the bowl of the Porch where a flaming upsurge of reds, violets, and earthy browns unfolded like petals of a gigantic rose.

The once egg-shaped cloud had now filled the immense space and we were inside it. Motes of gold spun around my head, singing in my ears, dotting my face. The vision made me light-headed. My ears tingled. My arms hung loose at my sides. The mallet slipped from my fingers and rested, handle-up on the deck beside my feet. And even though I'd stopped striking the bell, the spectacle didn't fade. It was as if Time itself had paused to marvel at this show of lights and sounds.

Then little by little the bell tones began to drop off.

The diamond lenses diminished in intensity and receded. Tandre and I looked on mesmerized, as button-sized stars looped away, playfully fizzing and popping in the air like effervescent bubbles. The room darkened and the cloud gently shrunk back to its original size in the center of the space.

Caspian's face reformed. His features distinct once again. He didn't speak for a long time.

"Forgive me," he finally said. "I'm speechless with delight. Magical bells indeed. I cannot begin to tell you what this means."

"I can," Tandre exclaimed. "It means we've sailed over the horizon and reached the hallowed shores of the angelic."

"The bell needs to be here, Jean. Not at the front door."

"Then here it will be."

"And bellmaker…" Caspian's eyes searched for me on the deck. "…what a gift you bring us. The tolling of your bell sets in motion a more evolved community of souls."

The tips of my body revved with electricity. Tandre looked over at me, jubilant, clapping his hands, then quickly turned back to Caspian.

"Charles, what if we set the bell under the bowl beneath the cloud?"

"Always the creative, Jean," Caspian said.

"I'll call you when we have it in place."

"Until then." Caspian's face melted into the mist.

I couldn't hold my elation a second longer. "Yow!" I howled without restraint. "Did you hear the lights?" I pointed high above the cloud. "Did you hear the song of the lights?!"

"Yes! Yes!" Tandre pumped his arms over his head ecstatically.

"Who were they?"

"The Ascended Masters, the Great Brotherhood. Who knows?" Tandre bounded over to me, his face dripping wet with sweat and tears. "But what I do know is you're a Godsend who has come to my doorstep at a most auspicious hour."

He hurled his arms around me and bounced me about the deck of the Porch in a spirited jig, singing some French ditty. I smelled alcohol on his breath as we whirled like dervishes until he stopped as abruptly as we'd started. He held me by the shoulders at arms length.

"Say it again," he said. "In the beginning…"

"In the beginning?"

"Yes."

"Oh, you mean, in the beginning was the vibe."

"The vibe, yes! We just matched their vibe! Master beings don't simply come to us when we call. No, we have to raise our vibratory level to resonate with theirs before they will even say 'hi' to us."

"High C," I said.

"How's that?"

"The bell. It came tuned to high C. Turns out, that key is perfect for this space."

"Perfect as a pine cone."

"Wait 'til Roe sees it," I said.

Tandre dismissed the thought. He rolled his eyes as

if to say Leonard Roe didn't deserve to be a part of it.

"Must hurry now." Tandre waved me over to the bell. "We need to move your bell down under."

We muscled the bell one step at a time down the stairs to the orchestra pit. A task for five men. Not that Tandre and I didn't first balk at the challenge. But it was as if our bodies had been given extra strength from the sonic spectacle we'd just experienced. And once we set our minds to it, we managed to lower the bell to the pit with only moderate strain. From there the bell dollied smoothly under the Porch floor.

"You're sure it won't upset the dynamics?" I asked.

"No, I'm not," he said. "I'm not sure of anything. But when you're given a chance to contact the Gods you try everything."

"Are they from the Fifth Station?" I asked.

"The Fifth Station? Where'd you hear that?"

"Caspian."

"Ha! The man maps the Afterlife like the London Underground. Best we not attach a number or a value to them, it will only scoreboard the glorious."

Following him back up the ramp, I asked, "Later, I can see Lucia, right?"

"Absolutely!" Tandre smiled, still exuberant. "You can see your Lucia as many times as you wish. But first the bell needs to be set up."

He asked that I suspend it in the center of the semi-circle of magnets under the cloud floor and to wait there for his return before ringing it.

"Now, there's something I need to do before they arrest me and throw away the key," he said.

I watched the man depart through the tunnel singing his child-like French melody.

A scintillating vibrancy still charged the air of the Porch as I rolled the timber, hardware and tools down the long winding ramp. It felt like I was breathing brand new oxygen into my lungs. If I hadn't witnessed the ultrasonic display with my own eyes and ears I'd have certainly passed it off as someone's drug-induced hallucination.

While assembling the scaffold, I heard a gargling wail, like someone drowning nearby. *"Help me! Help please,"* it cried.

Zt!

The crying stopped. The zapping sound came from directly behind me where the floor lit up with a bluish glow.

Pivoting, I came face to face with a Nansa only a couple feet away. I instantly dipped my head, not wanting to scare it off. Then I lifted an open palm in welcome like Gudrun had done. The Nansa idled in front of me, checking me out.

Close up, it reminded me of the blue ostrich feathers Lucia threaded into her artwork, only this feather stood six feet high and three feet wide at the middle. The Nansa's body wasn't entirely blue. It had a pale gold, translucent stem with bone-white filaments branching off. Its outer fringe tapered to fine, pink-violet tips like the soft fledges of an arrow. And at the base of its stem, multi-colored threads gracefully swayed, reminding me of those long strands of seaweed in a rolling tide.

The Nansa pivoted to one side. Its body thin as a sheet of three-gauge steel. Then it swiveled, facing me flat on and began to intensify its light. Its fine tips flickered and I wondered if that was the way it communicated. I'm about to say something lame like, 'Hi, my name is…' and so on, when I heard another distant, agonized scream, and with it, the Nansa sped off up the ramp where it zapped the Leaker and was gone.

"Okay, what just happened?" I asked out loud in a daze. I let out a long held breath and rubbed my hands together wondering if the Nansa did something to me while we faced each other.

Seems like it was simply introducing itself. Showing me the features of its body.

If it did anything to me, I didn't sense it. I shook it off and went about my work, assembling the scaffold with bolts and angle brackets. I could have used some help lifting the bell into place. It was hard enough simply keeping the bolts from being sucked out of my hands by the pull of the magnets. Didn't think to ask Tandre, and the extra strength I'd found earlier had withered away. I ended up slipping wedges under the rim of the bell and hoisting it up inch by inch with nylon ropes.

After a lot of grunting and cursing I finally raised the bell into position onto the scaffold about five inches off the floor. Then I wheeled all the tools and extra components under the base of the ramp, and ambled back to the bell where I waited for Tandre. I assumed he'd gone to tell Roe about the supernatural light show, or maybe he was finally handing over the elusive Porch plans he'd been hoarding. I didn't really know. Still, it was obvious to me that Roe would change his mind about the bell once he saw the celestial fireworks. He'd be a fool not to.

Exhausted, I sat cross-legged on the floor with my back against a piling and blew air on the busted blisters between my thumbs and forefingers.

Hanging there, with its profile backlit by the spotlights, the bell looked like a relic unearthed from some ruins in the Sahara desert. Its significance veiled in mystery.

Tandre's intuition felt right. Setting the bell directly under the cloud could give the tones even more potency. Dead center amidst the encircling magnets. I'd always bashed the notion that things were meant-to-be. Yet sitting there I couldn't deny the feeling in my gut that the bell had found its true home. And stranger still, that my arrival at the Sylvia House was not two months late, but somehow divinely timed.

And to think, it all began with a bullet.

Eleven years ago I found a handgun in the alley behind my studio. Someone must have ditched it or abandoned the weapon during a chase. I snatched it up and welded it into a sculpture. The gun added extra menace to an already offensive piece. And the sculpture sold fast. Which inspired me to go to the cops. I asked them for guns to work into my sculpture. Weapons they obtained in raids. They rejected me at first. Then some higher-up got wind of it. Figured I was going to make a statement. Anti-gun, anti-violence. Get in the news. Give them some positive buzz: Police Promote Peace with Art Piece. Not me. Been done to death. But I didn't tell them any different and they gave me a ton of confiscated guns. Bins of them. One officer even donated his own standard issue Glock, preferring another firearm.

My studio turned into a mini-arsenal. I didn't know the names of most of the weapons. Didn't care to. Just used them like any other material. Take them apart. Melt the metal down. Weld them en masse. Mobiles made out of revolver barrels. A free standing shotgun candelabra. The assault rifle chandelier I made is probably still hanging in that Berkeley biker bar.

In no time an attachment developed. I got to enjoy the feel of a gun in my hand. Even unloaded they had power. I started carrying the Glock the cop had donated. Took it to parties. Down to the corner café. Gave it a rub like a lucky charm. My little attack dog. Always at the ready. Tugging at the leash to let it have a say in things. Only a matter of time. Get a couple drinks in me. Piss me off. Watch out.

Sure enough the time came.

A blind abstract painter set up a meeting for me with a big art dealer. "Mr. International" they called him. I arrived at his garishly decorated Victorian in Pacific Heights late one night. The time had been pre-arranged but still the man kept me waiting over an hour. Every ten minutes his Latin lover would saunter giggling into the living room, refill my glass with Chardonnay and leave without a word. By the time

Mr. International finally appeared in a cloud of cigar smoke, with his hairy belly bulging over the sash of a silk kimono, I was boiling. He hurriedly flipped through the folder of photos I'd brought showing most of my work, all the while wiping his balding head with a small towel.

"I'll tell you straight up," he said. "You're like one of those Fourth of July sparklers that fizzle to death in seconds. Sure, you got some balls. A bit of flare. But no legs. You don't have it in you to go beyond being just a fizzer. And I don't take on fizzers like you so stop wasting my precious time."

And with that he flung the folder at my face and started to sidle away. Photos flew out of the folder like frightened pigeons and I snapped. No sooner did they hit the floor I had the Glock out, pointing at his head.

"Fizz on this, sleazebag!" I shouted.

Seeing the gun, Mr. International sputtered to his knees bleating and begging me not to shoot.

Didn't really matter whether I pulled the trigger or not when you get right down to it. Thoughts are actions, too. Real or intended murder, it's in the same tone family. I didn't know that then. I didn't know how the intent goes with you whether you do the physical harm or not. It burns back at both ends. That's the hell of it. I can still hear the man's cries of terror and see his piss pooling on the parquet floor.

A few months passed without any reprisals or police knocking on my door. No grievances were filed. Evidently Mr. International didn't want that kind of exposure. Fine with me.

Then one morning I stepped out of my studio into the street.

BLAM!

A shock of darkness swallowed me like a cave and sucked me down in its undertow. I didn't know I was unconscious, somersaulting in the clutches of death. All I knew was I was being tormented by a horrific specter. An endlessly long eel-like creature had its tentacle mouth attached to my chest and was dragging me through a rot-smelling void. Needle-sharp tongues darted out its mouth and corkscrewed into the arteries and veins around my heart like hungry feelers craving blood. I had no hands or arms to detach the thing from me. Powerless I plummeted, only to find more eely creatures snipping at my sides and I came to realize that the one gripping my heart was only a single arm of a much larger entity.

Ringing wet with sweat, I awoke from this madness in survival tremors, gasping. I'm in a hospital bed at San Francisco General. Grandpa Frank is standing at the foot of the bed.

"You got shot, Joe."

No need to guess who pulled the trigger. Everyone in the Bay Area art scene knew it was a sharp shooter the art dealer hired. The bullet missed my heart by a funky hair. Some sharp shooter.

Surgeons huddled and ended up refusing to extract the bullet.

"Too dangerous?" Frank confronted them. "What are you saying? And it's not dangerous where the sucker's lodged in there up against his ticker? Hell, you guys perform heart transplants every other Tuesday and you can't remove a stinking bullet?"

One morning I awoke to find a crimson felt thing flopped over the IV stand next to my hospital bed. A bizarre-looking feathered hat adorned with a shiny foil eye mask. Stitched to the hat's pointed top was a little bell. The hand painted card tethered to the fuzzy brim read: LET YOUR LIFE RING TRUE. L.K.

"You remember Lucia Kazan?" Frank asked me and described the woman.

"Yeah, I remember her."

"She made it."

Never wore the hat. But I became fascinated with the bell. An acorn-sized sleigh bell of sorts with a crude, square handle. It produced a muted jingle created by a couple pellets bouncing around its hollow. Turns out to be a crotal. One of the oldest types of bells known. I'd ring it in the hospital to annoy the nurses.

Funny thing is, the crotal spoke to me. I started to envision making metal sound sculpture. Not chimes, but gongs and bells. I could pull from those bins of firearms and build a big iron bell covered with melted guns sticking out. Call it, 'The Heavy Toll.' They'd dig that. Especially since it was made by the victim of a shooting.

Fortunately for me right across the bay in Emeryville was an old foundry. Its 68-year-old Master Founder, Benni Bonatti, had been casting bells and other works of art for nearly 50 years. I proposed my gunmetal idea to him and he agreed to take it on. Word spread. The city of Oakland heard about the bell and bought it for $125 grand. Blew me away. Most money I'd ever made on a piece by far. But once completed, the chamber of commerce couldn't find a site for it. Nobody wanted 'The Heavy Toll' fronting their building. And for good reason. The thing looked like a big black hulk of ugly, pimpled and barbed with barely recognizable gun parts. Plus, it gave off a flat, clunky clang when rung. Which is what you'd expect for such a thick-walled iron bell. The city ended up installing it outside a cinderblock detention center on some weedy back street lost among the littered desolation of scrap yards.

My life was all bells from then on. I locked up my studio to the public, stopped taking calls and dropped out of the art scene. People thought I was dead anyway and I did nothing to change their minds. My days and nights were spent at the Bonatti Foundry watching Benni and his crew at work, learning everything I could about bell making and casting.

Since I showed up everyday, Benni carved out time to educate me. I had no idea there were precise mathematical formulas involved in making bells that were passed down from father to son. That's how Benni started in Italy as a boy. Not having a math mind, it took me months to get my brain around it. But bell making is not all science, there's also an art. And that's where the ear comes in to play.

"You never play an instrument? How can you begin to understand?"

Benni would blindfold me and have me listen to all sorts of bells, chimes, xylophones, organs. He'd blow a pitch pipe in my ear and make me name the notes. He'd bong a bell and have me describe to him the changes in the journey of the sound.

"Most people only hear one big clang. But a good bell gives so much more. To be a bellmaker you must fine tune your ears to hear all the octave shifts from the initial strike sound to the partials, the harmonic overtones and the lasting hum tone."

And so I listened and learned.

"Light follows sound," Benni instructed. "So, if you wish to reach enlightenment, you first must reach ensoundment."

We argued a lot. I didn't want to make the tried and true. I wanted to take bells to another level both in form and composition— hourglass shapes, fuchsia shapes, scalloped shapes and wind funnels.

Bell bronze is mostly copper with a dash of tin. I'd propose different properties, like 'blass', a combination of glass with bronze filings. I searched for other minerals. Anything to enhance the sound. Infuse some new lab-modified aerospace alloy or pre-metal to create the sound of a ten-ton bell for a fraction of the weight and cost.

"Pre-metal?" Benni gave me a sour look. "You talk silly. You think you can improve on 5,000 years of bell making?"

"Lava."

"What?"

"Molten lava," I said.

"From a volcano?" Benni snatched his stainless steel thermos cup off a worktable, dumped the remains of cold coffee on the concrete floor and handed me the cup. "Here, take this to Mount Vesuvius. And hurry back fast. Got to have it red hot for the mold."

Even though Benni would droop his head in dismay or bowl over and laugh in my face, a part of him delighted in my explorations.

Two years of failure, I still pressed on. I never lost the rush of excitement the moment when the cast was breached and a new bell was born. Metal sculpture is one thing, but bells add the sound dimension. And not just one, but an entire spectrum of tones that I believed could realign bones, open folds in the brain, and even slow the aging process.

The bell tones definitely heightened my perception of the world. They intensified my senses as if they'd been asleep since birth. I began to see more vividly, hear more distinctly, and feel sensations I'd previously numbed out. Even my hot temper slackened off a bit.

So, I'd keep feeding Benni preposterous bell models I hand-built in plasticine. He'd look at me like an ignorant fool, dump the model in a trash barrel, and order me to stop bothering him.

A few days would pass with no word. Then I'd get a call from him. "Get over here."

Benni loved a challenge. It made him young again.

One day Grandpa Frank urged me to drive him to the opening of a show at a downtown gallery. I went along, surprised to see the show featured some of Lucia Kazan's feather sculptures and burlesque outfits. I'd never gotten back to her about the felt hat she made for me in the hospital, and yet for two years I'd carried that little crotal bell in my pocket. It replaced the Glock.

Without so much as a hello, I walked up to Lucia, opened my fist and showed her the crotal bell in the palm of my hand. "Remember this? It was attached to a hat you made that I found hanging beside me in Intensive Care."

"There it is." She smiled, first at Grandpa, then at me. "Frank told me you had risen from the dead."

"Where did you get this bell?"

"It's been in the family for eons," she said.

"It's called a crotal. Do you know how old it is? It could be in a museum."

"Oh that would be sad, locked in some glass cabinet and never jingled."

Right then I liked the woman. I asked her if I could buy her coffee sometime.

Only a few weeks after seeing Lucia, I hit a stroke of luck at Benni Bonatti's foundry. I haphazardly added a mix of high tech alloys to the copper on a small, torus-shaped bell I'd designed. The sound it achieved was astounding for the size of the bell.

Replicating the accident took months. We worked the mixture a number of ways on various samples at slightly different temperatures until we were ready to commit to casting a bigger one. And when we broke open the mold there it stood— a 100-pound bell that delivered a multi-octave scale as full, as long and almost as loud as one weighing a ton. Just one downside, the bell would maybe last ten years of use before losing its clarity or cracking.

So be it.

The upshot of all of our experiments with my unconventional bell shapes and accidental recipes resulted in the harmonic bell that hung in front of me under the cloud floor of the Porch. All because of a bullet and Lucia's little bell. Both of which I still carried with me.

Time ticked by. Tandre didn't show. I began to nod off when a tremor rippled my skin. Someone was talking out there.

Roe.

I knew his voice, sharp and steely with a certain ship admiral finality. It came from above me on the deck of the Porch, and with it a strained, high-pitched voice I didn't recognize.

I climbed the ramp and peered out from the darkness of the orchestra pit. Roe stood alone at the podium speaking to the face of a woman in the cloud.

"No, nothing's changed," he said.

"I'm telling you something's changed."

The woman in the cloud had a pretty face, a bird-like nose and penetrating eyes. Like Roe's eyes, intense as spinning drills.

"They re-tuned the magnetic plates," Roe said.

"There's been a shift alright. I can sense it. But go on, you were saying."

"I cut the staff down from forty-five to a dozen and doubled the number of security guards.

"And you got rid of the dog," she said.

"The dog has been removed."

Zt!

"Must get those plans, Leonard."

"I will."

"It's in his contract. Don't let that man manipulate you. This is paramount to our command."

"I know."

"You must obtain the final plans and patent them immediately."

"I've told you who I'm dealing with. Sometimes I just want to kill him," Roe said.

"Don't even think that. Just get those plans."

"For all I know he's destroyed them. Or they could be in his mind, making it up as he goes."

"You sound just like your father, evading the dirty work. Of course they exist. How else did this get built?"

"Well, I know he made some modifications as he went along."

"You will find those plans by all means necessary. Steal them if you must. Anything short of death, that is. We don't want him on this side. Whatever it takes, Leonard. Appeal to his grandiosity if you must."

"I wouldn't stoop. I have another lure already in motion."

"Then have a backup plan."

"Worst case, I'll hire engineers to take the entire Porch apart piece by piece, blueprint each detail and re-build it."

"Don't be absurd."

"I said 'worst case.' I'm confident my trap will take him out of the picture."

"Good."

Zt!

"Well, I better go. Our special guests have arrived and are about to get a tour of the grounds."

"Do they know why they were chosen?"

"No. They think it's an investment opportunity. I'll bring them in after dinner."

"Excellent. Soon the alliances will be solidified."

"Indeed."

"Don't bring the girl."

"Of course not."

"Have you picked out a school for her?"

"Yes. Outside London. Far enough away."

"And she knows?"

"She will soon enough."

"Then we will have it all, won't we Leonard. We will control both sides, and no one will access the Afterlife except through me."

"Yes, mother."

Zt!

I gulped for air.

Ray was right. They were taking it away from Caspian.

So much for angels and ascended masters.

Roe waited for the face of his dead mother to completely dissolve before leaving the podium.

The revelation rocked my body. I stood in the orchestra pit numb with shock, wondering what "lure" Roe had set up for Tandre. Whatever it was I needed to warn the man. I considered confronting Roe right there as he descended the ramp. Catch him naked in his power grab. But then what? Then I'd never see Lucia, that's what.

"*Agh!*" The tormented cry of a Leaker raided my ears. At the mouth of the tunnel a Nansa zapped it straightaway. Roe didn't respond. Hard to say if he could see these light beings given how he walked locked-step past it as if it was a beggar on the street.

Standing in the shadows, I waited for the suction gush of Death's Door to sound. I could've called for Lucia right then and there, but it didn't cross my mind. All I could think of now was finding the architect and blowing Roe and his mother's plot to kingdom come.

Emerging from the tunnel, I spotted the legs of a shadowy form in the mudroom.

"Someone left their cowboy boots here. I must've overlooked them when I came in."

Roe had faked his exit.

"A spy, yes?" he said.

He punched a round red button on the mudroom wall. Death's Door swooshed open with a burst of air. I half-expected to see Gorno and his goons storm in but all I saw were shafts of sunlight dappling the leaves of Eden.

"You need to hear the bell." I lifted my body out of the tunnel only to catch a fleeting glimpse of the burl knob of Roe's cane an instant before it collided with my head.

Smack!

The room whirled.

The next thing I heard was the clinking of ice cubes

in a glass. I'm seated in an Eames chair, staring down at my stocking feet, my head pounding like a piston. They'd removed my shop coat. Evidence I'd been searched while unconscious. I felt my pant's pocket for the little bell Lucia had given me. It was still there.

Around me, a cavernous space with a high ceiling. Big as it was, the room felt airless and oppressive. Raven-black walls, a hardwood floor with red throw rugs, and vases of red roses sitting on glass tables. Fastened to the walls were giant abstract paintings with ragged, red and orange crosses slashed across the canvas that looked like they were applied with a mop.

Before me, a long, sliding panel door half-open to an adjacent room where Roe stood in a starched white shirt facing a wall mirror the width of a bus.

I looked around Roe's gloomy lair. My eye sockets ached. I noted a door to my left. Pebbled glass. A blurry silhouette on the other side. Security guard, no doubt. Something in the room emitted a hollow moan. Looking around I spotted an oval shadow on the floor. This was no throw rug. This was a Leaker, vaporous and dark as an oil slick. And here I thought they were confined to the Porch.

So, where's the Nansa to zap it?

Chilled by the sight, I stood up, only to flop back into the chair, reeling. The pulsing lump on the side of my forehead hard as a chestnut.

"Ah," Roe said, eyeing me in the mirror's reflection. "The interloper awakes."

He set his drink on a bar counter and cinched the knot on his red necktie.

"Your brief time here is at an end. But before you go you're going to tell me all about your association with the architect and the devious deeds you and Ray Freely are cooking up."

"You're the devious one. You and your dead mother," I said.

"Don't tax me with your knothole view of things." Roe stiffened his back and lifted his chin in the mirror. I assumed he was prepping his looks and posture to impress the coming investors. "It's obvious your uninformed bias has blinded you."

"No, what's obvious is how you and your dead mother are stealing the portal to the Afterlife away from Caspian and his daughter."

Roe turned sideways. He pulled over a bar stool and sat on it, his pant cuffs bulging over his boots.

"Stealing? Quite the opposite. I'm saving it from annihilation. Do you even know who Charles Caspian is?" he said, his tone spiked.

I must have struck a nerve.

"I know if it wasn't for Caspian none of this would exist," I said.

"Don't be so sure." He lifted his left leg and rolled the pants up to the knee revealing a shiny prosthetic limb. "The architect was already on the verge of solving the trans-dimensional riddle. Only a matter of time. And funding."

Roe directed his fingers to a raised disk located just below the knee joint.

"And so the funding came from a man who had countless millions, yet gave none of it to his ex-wife and son. Not one red cent. And by red, I mean blood-stained."

He rotated the disk counter-clockwise.

"Surely you know how the man made all his money?" He depressed something next to the disk with his thumb. "No?" He answered himself, "I guess you don't. These things seem to get lost in the dazzling haze of the man's philanthropy."

A jet of steam hissed from the knee joint and Roe's artificial leg extended like a telescope.

"Weapons manufacture." Roe watched his leg grow until it reached the length he wanted. "Land mines to be precise. That's right, Charles Caspian invented a dud-proof antipersonnel land mine. Unique in how it could be calibrated by weight, allowing it to be buried a bit deeper in the ground than earlier versions. This made them less detectable yet no less sadistic."

He twirled the disk until tight.

"Land mines never sleep," he went on. "They lie there waiting for some fresh meat to come by. A child maybe. Or a mother. Could be Cambodia. Could be Mozambique."

He unrolled the pant leg. The cuff fit his longer leg length perfectly.

"They're everywhere, you know. All over the world. Hidden underfoot until ..."

BANG!

Roe stomped his left foot on the floor. The vibration prickled the low-lying shadow by the door.

"And this is the man for whom none of this would exist, you say. A man who spent the first half of his life making death traps and amputees."

As Roe repeated the same drill on his other stainless steel leg, I rubbed my head and considered the best way to get back at the man. The dormant hate and hostility of younger days churned under my skin, coiled to strike.

"Then comes the day when Caspian collides with his creation," Roe continued. "His karma, so to speak. There's an accident in his own backyard. His boy had absconded with one of his prototypes. Imagine, the man had never witnessed the atrocity of his own invention. And then what? An epiphany of the heart? Not even close. More like a deluge of guilt. The home accident sparks a surge of recurring nightmares. He can't shake the wailing cries of all the maimed and murdered out of his head. So, he drops everything. He leaves his wife and eleven-year-old handicapped son and vanishes. No one knows where."

Roe stood up on his longer legs and faced the mirror. Now a good six inches taller, six-foot seven or eight.

"Seeing more now? Your little knothole a bit bigger?" He raised his chest and stuck out his chin, high and regal, like a heroic statue in a city square. Then he let out a long exhale and continued his story.

"Years pass, and then one day Caspian resurfaces. A philanthropist now, with a foundation. Oh, but that doesn't wash the blood off his hands or quiet the rails of suffering in his ears. No, the nightmares will not cease, and he disappears once again."

Roe lifted a navy black suit jacket off a stool and

thrust his arms into its sleeves.

"Many years pass. He's an old man now with a little girl. A mystery child. And he's dying. He tries to make amends with those he's abandoned."

Roe took a few steps forward and back, adjusting his balance to conform to his new height.

"Wonderful word 'amends.' Sounds like 'amen,' yes? But in this case it fails to put closure to a hymn or a prayer. Instead it tears open a deep wound. So, to clean up his act, as they say, Charles Caspian starts on a new mission."

Roe picked up his cane and strutted into the room toward me looking like one of those carnival men walking on stilts high above the cotton-candy crowds.

"Which is the instrument we have here. Arguably the most phenomenal invention in human history. And yet there's a catch that's inherent to the man. You see, he can't stop creating minefields. And this one's going to blow up in all our faces unless..."

The door opened a crack. A face peered in.

"Dora, yes, please come on in." Roe waved for the person to enter.

In marched a stocky woman in a lab coat. The stone-faced nurse I'd seen at the celebration talking with Roe. She held up a ring of keys and a billfold and handed them to him. He smiled and ushered her into the adjacent room where he set the items on the counter and had her shut the sliding doors behind them.

Although muffled, I could still hear them converse.

"Excellent, Dora. All going as planned."

"Like an oiled engine," she said.

"And the Limbo Room?"

"Poised and ready."

"Here, take this," he said. "A modest reward for a job well done."

I tried standing again. My head a clang of chains. I shuffled across the room to the window. The same crooked third story window I'd seen Roe staring out when I first arrived.

And that was only yesterday.

On the ground outside, Julian walked along the path speaking to two men and a woman. The investors, I surmised.

Having heard Roe's story about Caspian being his estranged father, I started connecting the dots. Roe's greed was obvious. Seizing absolute control of the place would make him the richest man in the world. Tandre must have suspected it. Why else would he be so reluctant to turn over the plans for the Porch? It's not about some service contract. In his gut he doesn't trust this guy. But even without the takeover, Roe would still be bathing in billions. There must be something more to it than the wealth. And what did his mother stand to gain? Was there some kind of spiritual equivalent to money on the other side? Some superior status in being the Afterlife operator?

His dead mother's shrill voice played over and over in my mind— "Then we will have it all. Then we will have it all"— until the vibe behind their motivation rung in my bones.

So that's it. The driving force for her is revenge and total domination. And for him, it's to take the crown from his father's head and be the one and only King of the Dead.

The sliding door swished open and Roe and Dora stepped out.

"Gudrun? No, I hadn't heard," Roe said, scanning the room and finding me at the window.

"Nobody knows." Dora tucked a manila envelope under her arm.

"Oh, she must be around somewhere. Have you paged her?"

Dora gave me a suspicious glare followed by an eye check to Roe, who answered her with a swift jog of his head.

As they moved to the door, the low, shady mass of the Leaker eddied around their feet.

Neither took notice.

"Have a splendid journey," Roe said, opening the door for her.

Outside in the hallway stood the jowly, bulldog face of dead Janie's Dad, dressed in the blue uniform of a security guard.

Roe leaned over at the waist and set his hand on the man's shoulder. "I need to meet with our guests," Roe informed him. "While I'm away, find out everything you can about this man's dealings with Jean Tandre and Ray Freely. Every sneaky detail. He reeks of subversive scheming."

I pulled off my socks. The circumstances called for action, without delay.

As the guard mumbled something back to Roe, I slipped into the adjacent room and up to the bar, socks in hand.

"Get away from there," the guard ordered, entering the room.

"Hang on. I need ice," I said, filling a sock with hard cubes, "You see what he did?" I half-turned and pointed to the shiny bump on my forehead. "He cracked my skull with his ugly stick."

"You think that's an ugly stick. Wait 'til you get a shock of this."

The man lifted a shiny black two-foot long baton in his right hand and clicked a switch on its handle with his thumb. The club gave off an initial popping sound followed by a thrumming drone.

"Now get outta there," he commanded, advancing toward me waving the club back and forth like a metronome. "Unless you want to taste a few volts of a sizzle stick."

I dropped an ice cube on the floor.

"Oops."

The man took the bait. He leaned over to pick up the ice. As he did, I wheeled the sock overhead like a sling and whacked him across the temple with it.

He faltered.

I whacked him again.

He flopped to the floor.

"Here," I said, dropping the sock next to his body, "You're going to need that."

I yanked the electrified baton from the man's hand, grabbed my shop coat off a chair and headed out, barefoot. The Leaker I'd seen earlier lying by the door had gone.

"All going as planned." Roe's words came back to

me as I took the elevator down to the second floor.

And what was he saying about some stuff Ray and I were cooking up? News to me. And where'd Tandre go? Shit! Talk about a turn of events-- from light beings to dark deception in what, an hour?

From the top of the staircase I scanned the lobby. A different lobby. Newly redecorated. The aquamarine floor partially covered with Turkish rugs. Here and there glass coffee tables and planters set among leather sofas and chairs I'd seen the day before in Tandre's office.

No Camie at the reception desk. No one anywhere. They'd even shut off the waterfall that had plunged in a column from the top of the glass dome. The once bustling lobby had become silent as a knife.

Stepping onto the lobby floor, a voice crackled over the intercom, "Gudrun, please call Dora. Gudrun, call Dora right away."

A tattle of voices came from the design studio. Thinking it might be Tandre, I peered in, only to do a double take. No more drafting tables or architectural cabinets. The studio had been made over into a conference room. A long, glass table dominated the space. The model of the house was propped in the middle of it on a raised platform. Around the table in high-back chairs sat the two men and the woman I'd seen outside. All eyes were on Roe and Julian who stood next to a flip chart with their backs to the door.

"Now, as Julian might have mentioned during your tour, the exterior will be getting a face lift," Roe explained. "Here's an artist's rendering of the new facade. You'll notice how it's still in keeping with the traditional Heartland style."

I didn't hesitate. I jogged down the corridor toward the north door where Gudrun and I had parked the ATV and forklift earlier. But before I reached the door Julian's voice echoed behind me.

"Hey, psst, you there, hold up."

I stopped. Debated a second. I couldn't walk away from a chance to stick it to him. And I mean stick it to him with the baton I carried at my side.

"Julian." I swung around. "Are you involved in this piracy?"

Recognizing me, his eyes hardened. He came toward me, sucking air through his mouth, his stiff arms tight at his sides.

"Are you involved in this?" I repeated.

Not that I doubted Julian's involvement. I just wanted to see the expression on his face the moment he realized I knew what was happening.

"Simple yes or no question."

"I don't know what you're talking about. Do you?" His voice was breathy and hushed.

"I'm talking about your boss stealing what belongs to Caspian and his daughter. What do you have to say about that?"

"I'd say you been bonging too many bells."

"Really? Well, why don't you and I go ask Mr. Roe in there what I know, or better yet, his mother."

"Why don't we take this outside."

"What's wrong with right here?"

He made a move toward me. I lifted the baton and clicked the lever on the handle. Its wurr-wurr groan resounded off the walls of the corridor.

Seeing the sizzle stick, Julian's head tilted back like it was spun out of orbit. "Where'd you get that?"

"Found it lying around."

Julian jammed his right hand into his sport coat, only to realize his handgun wasn't there.

"Ah, must've ditched your weapon for your special guests." I stepped toward him, slicing the air with the baton like a sword.

"Okay-okay, let's be cool." He glanced back over his shoulder down the corridor. "We're just talking here, right?"

"I don't know, are we?"

"You want your bell, is that it?"

I didn't answer.

"And how about we toss in some traveling money for you? Some shopping money, huh? Get some decent clothes. A haircut. Stop looking like a bum."

"Keep your money. I just want to speak to a dead friend."

"Yeah, well I'd have to run that by the head honcho. He paused. "But I think it's doable."

I knew he was playing me. Last thing he wanted was for me to make a scene. Scare off the guests. A voice inside my head was shouting, *'You're wasting time. Go and find Tandre!'*

Julian backed up a couple steps.

"You wait right there. I'll see what we can do to get your needs met."

"Oh, and get me my boots."

Julian glanced at my bare feet. His face went blank. He made a gun with two fingers pointing it at my head. "And in return, you're going to get in your car and get outta my sight."

I got out of his sight all right. As soon as Julian left I sprinted out the north door. The ATV and forklift truck were gone. So, I headed up the hill on foot, skirting the gravel road, and clambering under the cover of the trees.

Big mistake. The fallen pine needles punctured the flesh of my feet with every step. I wanted to stop but I knew Julian would have guards on my tail within minutes. I continued climbing up past the barn to Tandre's silo. A Jeep sat outside. I listened for carts and the footfalls of people chasing after me. All I heard was the piercing chant of a cardinal in a nearby tree.

I stopped in the walkway outside the silo. The bottoms of my feet were caked with dirt and blood. I plucked out a couple pine slivers, then hobbled to the front door. I could hear a splashing, water-spilling sound and someone moving inside. When I reached for the door, it opened part way. Gorno's face peered out. He was dressed in a black sport coat and turtleneck, a nametag pinned to his lapel: T. Gorne.

"Looking for someone?" he asked.

"Yeah, I am," I said. "Just not you."

Gorno set something down behind the door and lumbered outside toward me.

"I need to talk to Jean Tandre."

"Oh, you do, do you?"

I retreated a few steps from the brute, lifted the electrified baton and flipped on the switch.

"Back away from me man," I warned.

He didn't.

"Where'd you get the sizzler?" he said, and lunged at me.

I sidestepped his grasp and stabbed his upper arm with the point of the baton. I could feel a jolting surge of electric volts shuddering in my hand. But his face showed no sign of shock or pain. He just stared for a moment at the coil of black smoke rising from his coat. Might as well have been a child's toy in my hand.

"Now look what you done." Gorno nabbed me by my scalp. "Burnt a hole."

He curled my body backward until it felt like my spine was going to snap like a stick.

"Drop it," he said.

I let go the baton. It clattered on the walkway.

He stood me back up and muscled me to the Jeep.

"So, where's Tandre?"

"Last I saw he was taking a nap."

"Well, we've got to wake him up right now!"

"Why's that?" Gorno cuffed my hands with zip-ties and loaded me into the passenger seat.

I tried to explain what I'd seen in real simple terms as though he was new to the house. I told him about Charles Caspian, about the bell I'd made, and about Roe and his dead mother seizing control of the Porch."

"What porch? What the hell you talking about?"

"The place where you can speak to dead people.

The Afterlife, man!"

It didn't register.

"Got your dude here. Be right down," he informed someone on his walkie-talkie. Then he fastened my hands to the grip on the dashboard.

"Do you get what's going on here?"

He wasn't tracking a word I said. The way they kept people in the dark, why was I surprised? He may have never been inside the Porch for all I knew. Either that or he was a one-way soldier. In it for the paycheck, right or wrong.

"It's all bad, man. It's a mutiny and you're in it."

He spun the Jeep around. We sped down the hill. Along the road and moving among the trees security guards roamed, hunting for me.

"What, are you some kind of mercenary?" I asked.

"I done that," he said.

"I believe it."

Partway down the hill to the house, his walkie-talkie, cradled in the Jeep's console, barked. Gorno pressed the speaker button.

"Yeah?"

"Gorno, it's Speed, over."

"What now?"

"Gotta situation here."

"What kinda situation," Gorno said.

"Some berserk old pastor."

"A what?"

"Can you get over to the gatehouse?"

"I was on my way there."

"Good. And where is everybody? They hire extra

security and I get no help."

Gorno punched a button, killing the connection.

We rounded the last bend and pulled up to the front of the house where Julian stood blocking the path, smoldering.

"Like nailing jello to a wall," Julian said to Gorno. He turned to me with jittery, maniacal eyes. "But you're busted now. And here's your ticket out."

He pushed a paper-clipped document past my face and into Gorno's hands. I recognized the pages from the legal documents I'd seen but never signed.

"See that Mr. Gandy here autographs this at the gatehouse and have Speed notarize it."

"Done," Gorno said, setting the paper-clipped pages in his lap.

"You say one word about this place, or even think about it, our attorneys will bury you. And if I see your face anywhere near here…" Julian grinned and opened his sport coat to expose the handgun he'd retrieved, "… it'll be your pain and my pleasure."

"What about my bell!"

"You blew your chance, Ding Dong."

"Yeah?" I twisted my cuffed hands and aimed two index fingers at him. "If I don't get my bell and all my stuff back it will be your face whining from that cloud of death."

"Send us a bill," he hissed in my ear. "And here," he cocked his head back, hocked up a lugee and spat it on my face. "You can use that to lick the stamp."

Gorno stomped on the gas. The Jeep cut across the clay path, churning up the edges of the newly laid sod.

I looked back at the Sylvia House, wiping the phlegm off with the sleeve of my shop coat.

"It's a conspiracy!" I sounded off, hoping the investors might hear me. "They're stealing it all away from… "

Before I could holler Caspian's name, Gorno let go of the wheel and backhanded me in the mouth so hard it jarred my teeth and split my lip.

"Anything more you want to say?"

"Yeah, plenty, but no one wants to hear it."

Gorno drove the Jeep under the arbor and skidded to a stop at the glass doors of the gatehouse. He took out a switchblade, cut me loose from the handgrip and pushed me inside, my wrists still cuffed.

Speed, the gatekeeper, stood with his back to us. He was talking to an irate man who paced back and forth outside the receiving window. At first I thought the guy must be one of Roe's guests. A late arrival.

Not the case.

"What's the trouble?" Gorno said.

Speed spun around. He wore the same blue nylon windbreaker he'd worn when he signed me in the day before.

"Gorno! Hey, look at you, all dappered up with a sport coat and what's that, you even got a nametag."

"Who's the dude?" Gorno joggled his head toward the man outside.

"He's some pastor from Newgrange who insists his daughter is here."

"Let me deal with him."

Speed punched a button on the counter by the window. A buzzer sounded.

"No, no, don't let him in!" Gorno blurted.

"Oops." Speed frowned.

Through the gatehouse door came a cross between Moses and Buffalo Bill. The man had chalk-white shoulder length hair, a long white beard and bushy eyebrows. He wore a buckskin jacket with fringe down the arms. In his right hand he clutched one of those tall, hardwood staffs— the kind they use in martial arts.

"Why would they leave a message to pick her up if she was never here?" The Pastor beat his staff on the floor. His eyes wild and red. Spittle glinting in the hairs of his beard.

"I'm head of security," Gorno said, stepping up to the counter with me in tow. "What's all this about?"

"Like I explained to this man. My daughter came here this morning and…"

"I told him that everyone has to sign in," Speed interrupted. "And she's not in the register."

"What's her name?" Gorno asked the man.

"Sarah Magnuson."

That's the woman whose child drowned.

Speed handed the register book to Gorno.

"See for yourself. No one by that name signed in. The only people signing in today were the money people and their limo drivers."

"Someone called us." The Pastor shook his stick. "They left a message to come and pick her up."

"And they told you to come here, to the Sylvia House?" Gorno asked the man while his eyes scanned the register book.

"The caller didn't leave her name. She gave us

directions to the place at the old Skogen Farm and..."

"Okay, okay. Hold on there, mister-er-Pastor-sir," Gorno cut him off. "One thing at a time. Got a little business to take care of first. Speed... " Gorno set the paper-clipped documents on the counter and pointed at me. "I need you to handle some exit paperwork on this guy here."

Speed looked me over. "What happened to him?"

"Never mind. You got that notary stamp of approval handy?"

"Sure do." Speed skittered like a mouse over to his desk and jerked open a drawer.

Out in the Jeep, the walkie-talkie squawked. Gorno ignored it.

"Okay, Ding Dong," he said, tugging me by my cuffs over to the counter. "Time to sign you out."

Speed set a notary stamp on the counter and opened the lid on an inkpad.

"I'm not signing nothin'," I said. "Not until I get my bell and tools back."

"That's it!" the Pastor said. "I'm going in and see for myself if Sarah's here."

"Hold on." Gorno raised a finger. "Nobody's goin' nowhere."

"She was here," I declared.

"You shut up." Gorno commanded.

The Pastor looked at me. "My Sarah?"

"Yes," I said.

"You saw her?"

"She came in the back gate."

Gorno rammed his elbow into my nose, dropping

me to the hard plank floor.

"Say another word and I'll flatten your face so hard you'll have to breathe through your asshole."

Stunned, the Pastor shouted, "What are you doing? Why did you strike this man?"

"It's best you stay out of our disciplinary affairs."

"You do not want to mess with me. Not today," the Pastor warned Gorno. "You will let the man speak. He claims to have seen my daughter."

"He lies." Gorno said. "He saw nothing and nobody."

The pain in my nose ignited a surge of adrenalin. My body automatically kicked into kill mode. Seeing my face redden, Gorno squared up.

"Whoa, you want a piece of this?"

More than just a piece. I wanted the whole thug. Lucky for me another option availed itself.

He propped me up against the counter. Blops of blood dripped from my nose and splatted on the papers I was supposed to sign.

"Now look what you've done!" Speed nervously slid the papers out from under my face and searched the office for something to wipe off the blood.

The Pastor tapped me on the arm with his staff.

"Truly, you were with my Sarah?"

"That's it!" Gorno howled, attempting to put the kibosh on it. "We're done." He pointed at the Pastor and then at the door, "You musta got a crank call. Now get back into your car and back to your pulpit."

"If you don't let this man speak, I'll have the Sheriff of Newgrange out here with every patrolman in Sumac County!"

"Woo, you got my boxer shorts bunching up." Gorno said. Then he pressed his forehead against mine and muttered, "You say one more word…"

"There, I cleaned off the blood." Speed proudly skip-stepped back to the counter with the documents. "Magic of 7-UP."

"Go on." The Pastor jutted his chin at me. "When did you see Sarah?"

"This morning. I took her inside the house," I said.

Gorno thrust down on my cuffs, forcing me to my knees. Murder in his eyes.

Gorno knows something about the woman. Maybe he saw her, too.

"Speed!" he roared.

"Yeah?"

"See the Pastor man to his car."

The phone rang on Speed's desk.

"Hang on." Speed set the papers on the counter and went for the phone.

"Gatehouse. Yes sir, he is. Hang on. Hey, Gorno, it's the boss man."

Gorno let go of me. He leaned over the counter and pulled the phone out of Speed's hand.

"This is Gorne. No, not yet. Got him right here." He glared down at me on the floor. "Uh-huh, will do."

"Enough of this nonsense!" The Pastor tamped his staff on the floorboards and marched out the glass doors and down the arbor path toward the house.

"Hey!" Gorno fumbled with the phone. "Shit!" It slipped out of his fingers and plunked on the counter. "Speed!"

"The papers are right there, ready to sign."

"Screw the papers! Stop the Pastor!"

Speed jostled around the counter and hurried out the gatehouse after the man. "Hey, hold up there! Sir, you're trespassing!"

Gorno grabbed me by my collar and dragged me to the open door. "Change of plans, Ding Dong."

"How's that?"

"We're goin' back to the house."

"To get my bell?"

"Yeah, to get your bell rung." Gorno grinned. First time I'd seen his teeth. Little ground-down stumps.

The Pastor strutted on the path toward the house, and called back, "I warn you, try to stop me and I'll strike you down!"

Speed jogged up behind the man. Then in one swift karate motion the Pastor squatted, wheeled around with his staff and staggered Speed with a swat across his Adam's apple.

Seeing Speed flop to the ground, Gorno let go my cuffs and kicked me in the ribs so hard I toppled backward, slamming my head against a stack of unopened boxes of surveillance cameras.

"You move and I'll cripple you." Gorno crouched down, lifted a pant cuff, unsnapped a handgun from an ankle holster and charged out, shouting at the Pastor, "Freeze or I will shoot!"

"You don't know who you're dealing with," the Pastor spat through clenched teeth.

Speed lay at his feet, gripping his neck, writhing in breathless pain.

I forced myself to my feet, blood burbling out my nose. I stumbled around the counter, grabbed my truck keys off the key rack on the wall and heaved my body out the door to the parking lot, my brain in a fog. I scrambled past a couple limousines to my truck. Got in, stomped on the accelerator and tore out of there, gasping and groaning.

Where was I going? Anywhere fast. Just get free and away. Put as much distance as I could between me and the rhino.

It's not an easy trick maneuvering a stick shift with cuffed hands, but I managed. I figured Roe's ruffians would soon be chasing after me. Not that I could tell. All I could see were swirls of dust spewing up behind me as I high-tailed it out of the hills, going over in my head what had just transpired.

Was that Roe on the phone telling Gorno to take me back to house? What's that about?

I went over a number of scenarios.

Were they planning to buy me off to keep my mouth shut? Torture me? Hell, Gorno already did that.

It didn't make any sense at the time. Not that I hadn't witnessed more weirdness than any one person could swallow in the last 24 hours. Still, I never, ever, would've guessed the ghoulish maneuver they had in store for me.

The truck shuddered down the washboard road. Even with every inch of my body aching, I felt a ticklish satisfaction at being a thorn in Roe's side. Someone out in the world who knew about his secret deception. Someone who hadn't signed any ridiculous legal papers. Someone who would haunt his days and nights. I'd become the hitch in his universe.

The bouncing of the truck smoothed out. My ears picked up a sudden auditory shift. The dirt road had just turned to asphalt. I'd reached the outskirts of Newgrange.

Gearing down, I took the first right onto a narrow, dead end street and shut off the engine. My body shaking. I looked back, watching the dust slowly settle. No sign of anybody following me. No movement at all.

I squinted at my reflection in the rearview mirror— cheeks streaked with blood and snot, a split bottom lip swollen twice its size, and a bruised nose that would not stop throbbing or bleeding. I stanched it with everything I could find lying around the cab— maps of Montana, Minnesota and Wisconsin.

In the glove compartment I found a pair of pliers and used them to clip the zip ties around my wrist. Behind the seat I pulled out a wadded-up T-shirt. I tottered out of the truck, shed my shop coat and shirt, wiped my face and slipped on the black T-shirt. I felt parched, hungry and violent.

The side street where I parked was dead quiet. Looking around I saw that I'd stopped next to a little cemetery. I hobbled up a slight incline through grass and graves to a solitary oak tree. My ribs stung with every breath. Then came a gnawing ache in my chest on the left side of my heart. The dark side.

Not the old bullet.

Talk about land mines. I'd been carrying one inside me for ten years. The doctors warned me the bullet might someday come dislodged. Thanks to the heel of Gorno's shoe, it felt like it just did.

Given the shape I was in, my next move seemed obvious. Cut my losses and get to the nearest medical facility. Heal up and go west. Once home, I'd find a way to get my bell and tools back. With what I knew, I had plenty of leverage. I could threaten Roe if need be. Seemed like the best plan, except one thing— I didn't want to leave. Not after seeing Lucia's face. Not after witnessing the mind-boggling brilliance of those light beings.

Feverish and woozy, I lowered my body to the ground and leaned my back against the oak tree. The silent cemetery looked like it came straight out of an old western movie. The headstones all chipped and weather-beaten. Some tilted sideways in the dirt, the marble pitted, stained by lichen and time.

Good place to die, I chuckled to myself, holding my chest.

A bank of gray clouds pushed across the sky out of the west. As its shadow crawled up my legs and blotted out the afternoon sun I thought about Lucia's gravesite in Marin and the day she was buried. That was a gray day, too. And I recalled what Pearl, Lucia's art instructor and mentor, said at the funeral. Pearl wore one of Lucia's zany headdresses. Her white, stringy, steel wool hair stuck straight out from under the heap of feathers and stars, making her look like a clownish witch.

"You know," Pearl said in a husky voice, "Our snapshots of death are decorated with dreadful furnishings. The word itself conjures up such morbid and wretched images it's no wonder people become so gloomy and fearful around it. Yet, what do we truly know about this exit? Absolutely nothing. We paint images about it out of our loss, and pump the bodies with chemicals to stall Nature's composting job so the deceased can decay fashionably late. Yes, Lucia's life was cut short. And if given the power to shift the course of past events, it'd be the first thing I'd change. The sting is unbearable. But Lucia's life was plenty long enough for her to express her art and share her love. Which is more than most can say. It was long enough for her to belong in our hearts. Some would say this crazy hat of hers I'm wearing does not belong here at a funeral. Well, Lucia tells us it does. And I say to Death, resist all you want, in no time Lucia will find a way to belong in your heart, too. And then you won't be some dark and dismal place. No, you'll be fancifully adorned, resplendent and brash with spangles and wreaths of stars and flying feathers."

So absorbed by the memory of Pearl's speech, I didn't hear the car pull up. It wasn't until the footsteps thumped a few feet from my ears that I jolted to my senses.

"You all right?" the Pastor asked.

"No." I blew out a ragged sigh. "Not even close."

The old man looked me over. He offered me his handkerchief. I wiped my bloody nose with it.

"I see they convinced you to leave," I said.

"With a pistol to my head."

"Yeah, well, I saw how you leveled that gatehouse guy."

"They forced my hand," he said. "After seeing how they beat you I snapped. So, I struck the man. It seemed the only language they understood."

"Do you have any water?"

He came back from a rust-fendered Cadillac with a can of Fanta. It was warm but it quenched my thirst.

"What did you do to incite such a beating?" he asked.

"I refused to sign some papers," I said, keeping it simple. "I don't make promises."

"Well, in that you and I are alike."

He then confessed that he was no longer an acting pastor.

"There were complaints from the townsfolk. 'He's too Old Testament,' they said. 'A raving zealot.' They demanded I promise to soften up. Go easy on the congregation. I would not make such a promise. So they petitioned for my removal. Turns out, I've mellowed a bit. But don't tell them that."

"I won't," I said.

"Promise?"

I already liked the old guy.

"So, now I'm known around here as the Past-Pastor."

"The Past-Pastor," I muttered, and taking a labored breath, I clenched my teeth and stood up.

"Look, I know where your daughter was, but I don't know where she is now."

"You said you were with her."

"I escorted her into the house." I weighed my words. I really didn't want to be the one to tell him about Sarah's drowned little girl.

"The woman on the phone asked for us to come and pick her up and..." The Past-Pastor paused. His lips pursed. Then it spilled out. "I volunteered. I needed to be the one to tell her about Katie, her daughter." He choked up. "How... that they found her body..."

A shockwave swayed my head. I looked at the man's face. Vein-riddled hands cupped his mouth. Tears squirted out his clenched eyelids.

"In the river?" I said. "By the big willow?"

The Past-Pastor erupted with wrenching sobs. I handed the handkerchief back to him.

It's one thing to hear the girl speak from the cloud on the Porch and another to hear about the physical reality of her death. If I wasn't so pissed and pained I'd have wept right along with him.

"How did you know?" he said.

I balked. But it was too late. I couldn't take it back. He closed into me.

"How did you know where my granddaughter drowned?"

After a long hesitation, I shared what I thought the man could hear about my encounter with Sarah and her daughter, Katie.

The Past-Pastor was taken aback.

"What do you mean Katie told you about it?"

"Like I said, her soul spoke." I took short strides on my swollen feet. I needed to be moving to explain it.

"How can that be?"

He looked as incredulous as I must have when Caspian's face first formed in that misty cloud. We strolled side by side through the long grass among the graves.

"I know it sounds unbelievable, but it's true. The place is built to allow visual and audible transmissions between the living and the dead."

"You can actually see the deceased?" he asked.

"Clearly. Large as life."

The Past-Pastor stopped at a grave with a tall stone cross. I prepared myself for a fiery, fear of God sermon righteously punctuated with passages from the Bible. But, to my surprise, he embraced the idea.

"If true, then this is blessed news," he said. "There's been a rash of rumor and speculation around town about this cult of strangers from the East Coast and the mysterious goings on at the old Skogen farm. But nothing along these lines. So tell me, how do they do it?"

"Big magnets."

"Magnets?"

"Not the kind you stick to your refrigerator. These are the size of truck tires."

We walked on. The ache in my heart was not easing up.

"You're saying Sarah knew that Katie had drowned and went to the house to speak to her soul?"

"No-no. She didn't know Katie had drowned. The child had gone missing."

I shared with him what I heard on the Porch. How relieved Katie sounded when she heard her mother wasn't angry with her for going to the river, and how utterly devastated Sarah looked when she left. I assumed to go home.

"She didn't come home. She must still be on the grounds."

"I doubt that. They're evacuating everyone including the architect who master-minded the whole thing."

We came to the end of the cemetery and stopped at a knee-high picket fence, its white paint flaking off. The Past-Pastor sighed, lifted his head and shut his eyes.

"What did I know? All the times I've consoled those who'd lost dear friends and relatives to sudden and shocking deaths. I had no idea how it felt until now. It's..." He paused, shaking his head.

"Like being buried alive." I finished his sentence.

He swiveled around to face me. "You know it."

"My girl friend," I said.

"I'm sorry to hear that. Were you able to speak with her soul?"

"No. But I'd give anything."

He nodded. We walked back through the graves.

"In a blink, my granddaughter's gone," he said. "There's no time for any transition to elapse. Not even a minute to express the love I feel."

"And that's the amazing thing. With this place you can."

"So you say." He pointed to the names on a couple headstones. "So I could speak directly to Lillian Schmidt here, or Olaf Torgenson if I wanted to?"

"Would you prefer talking to them through a

psychic with a crystal ball or face to face?"

He didn't reply.

"I wish I could take you there," I said. "I wish you could see your granddaughter's face and hear her sweet voice. But it's not going to happen."

"They make it impenetrable don't they. And why? Why all the secrecy and brutality?"

The urge to tell him about the conspiracy was on the tip of my tongue. But it seemed too involved. Besides, it wasn't going to bring his granddaughter back.

"Control," I said. "Think about it. Try to count all the money. It's incalculable. Whoever owns such an extraordinary instrument will swim in riches without limit."

"I'd pay handily to see Katie. Just name the price. If only to say goodbye."

The Past-Pastor coughed and went silent, pondering.

When we reached the oak tree I heard him mutter, "Then again, this instrument you speak of may not be such a blessing afterall."

"How's that?"

He wiped the corner of an eye and lifted a finger.

"Our species is highly inventive. We froth over with fabulous concoctions and gadgets. And yet we create without considering how our shadow demands a share of each thing we make."

He pointed to the farm fields that extended beyond the cemetery.

"Whether its pesticides, nuclear power or the latest technological gizmo. The shadow is there, powerful and fierce with deadly consequence. And do we fear its power? No, we call it progress and leap into the froth. And now this amazing instrument you describe. To control such a conference of souls, this is truly God's turf."

"I don't know about that. But the way they're seizing it is diabolical."

"My point. That's the shadow doing its dark work."

A car rushed past on the main road. The Past-Pastor and I heard its urking grind of brakes and watched the vehicle back up and come toward us. Fear of Gorno puckered the skin on the back of my neck.

Then I saw it was a cop car.

"It's okay," the Past-Pastor said. "It's Howard, the sheriff."

While the Past-Pastor spoke with the sheriff at his patrol car, I sat on the top of a tombstone sipping the last of the Fanta and picking pine needles out from between my toes. The ache in my chest had lessened a bit. Every so often the sheriff would look over at me then look back at the Past-Pastor, the engine running all the while.

At one point, a dark van came cruising around the corner and immediately stopped. I made out two figures sitting in the front seat staring at us. The sheriff eyed them in his side mirror. After a couple seconds of idling there the van made a u-turn and drove off.

A short while later the sheriff left and the Past-Pastor came back.

"What is your name?" he asked.

"Joe Gandy."

He plucked a small notepad from his buckskin jacket and jotted something down. "Well, Joe Gandy, you're more than welcome in my home. Here is the address. I'd take you there myself but I must go. My daughter has still not returned. There are plans in the works. I hope you understand."

If he was implying something, I didn't catch it.

He started toward his car then made a swift about-face.

"I'm sorry to hear about your girlfriend," he said. "Death breaks our hearts but it also awakens us to the sanctity of Time. And Time is one thing rich and poor share alike. It's also the most undervalued natural resource." He swept his arm in a wide arc spanning the entire world. "Look around and see how Time suffers our apathy and neglect. We ravage it with distraction. Folks talk about making quality time. That's a hoot. Does it mean the rest is unworthy? Is not every instant treasure enough to open our hearts to the god within? 'Be here with all that you are,' Death reminds us with every life it takes away. 'Be in the raw, joyous and painful adventure of your heart while it beats."

The Past-Pastor drew a strained breath through his nostrils. He placed his hands on my shoulders. His heavy, red-rimmed eyes bore into mine.

"And are we in that adventure of our hearts right now or are we waiting for the time to be right? No, let Katie and your girl friend's death shake our cages and our comforts, and shock us deeper into life. There is no better time than this. We must be bold, Joe Gandy, for this day may be our last!"

His hands dropped from my shoulders.

"Alright, so I haven't mellowed afterall." He took the empty Fanta can out of my hand. "Recycle," he said and strode off to his car.

On the note the Past-Pastor handed me was an address in Newgrange. Under it he printed: COME EAT - CLEAN UP – REST & MEND.

What stayed with me as he wheeled away in his beat-up Cadillac was what he said about the shadow. I thought of Roe's mother and how the dead cast their shadows on the living. Tandre's instrument needed to be in the proper hands all right, only not ours. Not humans. It needed to be under the direction of those light beings I'd seen inside the Porch.

That's what I believed at that moment. Now I see it differently. Light beings have no experience riding the slow mule of the physical world. Just as human beings are unaware of the supersonic timing of the spirit realm. Best the instrument be governed by neither one nor the other, but a union of both, as Tandre inferred— the united state.

As I ambled out of the graveyard the jingling of the truck keys in my hand reminded me of Ray's pouch of keys hidden in the barn. Keys that would put me inside the house.

"Gitcha into everywhere," he had said.

I could sneak into the Porch before they changed the pass code. I could see Lucia before Roe and his mother hijacked the bridge between the worlds.

Turning the truck around, I pulled up to the T at the

main road.

To the right— the smart move. The Past-Pastor's place in Newgrange, warm food and rest.

To the left— a last chance to see Lucia.

Grandpa Frank's words came to mind, "The past is stupid. The future is wise. And the present is a tug of war between the two."

Night was darkening the land as I pulled up to the southern gate where I'd seen Tandre enter that morning. Spotting a video camera propped on a pole above the fence, I drove on another hundred yards. Parked my truck in a gully hidden from the road.

Perched on the chain link fence, two crows bobbed and cawed at me before flying off. I put my shop coat on to protect my arms. Then I removed the rubber floor mats from the cab and stashed the truck keys under a rear tire.

The ten-foot high fence appeared shorter from the road than when I stood at its base. Scaling to the top took everything I had. I slung the floor mats over the razor wire and cinched them with bungee cords. Then carefully I pitched my body over the top and monkey-swung to the ground with only a few shallow slashes in my wrists and hands.

Making my way up the grassy hill I smelled smoke. Not the odor of burning wood or charcoal briquettes. Something else. Above my head a black column of smoke spiraled into the low clouds. My first thought was a trash fire in the fire pit at the farmhouse. But the smoke didn't come from there.

Reaching the shoulder of the hill I froze in my tracks. Before me roared an ominous sight. Tandre's silo ablaze with orange flames lashing at the windows. Even though its brick walls contained the roaring fire like a burning kiln, from twenty yards away the heat baked my skin.

What the hell is this?

Two silhouettes stood at some distance from the inferno. I didn't recognize them from the back. I angled off toward the cover of trees as the fire took the shake roof. For a minute the silo looked like a giant Roman candle shooting flames and sparks straight up into the night sky. Ashes and bits of charred shingles rained down. Then a bone-cracking noise splintered the air as a floor caved and collapsed. This fire had rage behind it.

Why torch Tandre's place?

I didn't stick around to find out. I headed for the barn only to find it padlocked. I stumbled around looking for another way inside but found none. My plan to use Ray's stashed keys had hit a dead end. I was about to go down to the house without them when I heard a sneezing sound, and in the firelight I saw Barney, the raggedy cat, slink out of the barn through a hole in the siding. He was hacking up a hairball or something caught in his throat. A closer look revealed a cracked board where Ray had crashed the golf cart the night before in his drunken fury.

After working the board loose, I weaseled my body through the opening and headed straight for the stairs. The keys were still hidden under the bottom step. I cupped the pouch and stuffed it into my coat pocket. Then I made my way down the hill to the house hugging the shoulder of the road, my ears on high alert. I knew guards would be patrolling the grounds so I stopped often, listening for any snap of a twig or stir of gravel, ready to jump into the shadows or jump on them.

I reached the side door of the house without incident. But key after key failed to fit the slot. As my fingers fumbled for the last key on the carabineer, a motor started up. It sounded like a generator or the diesel engine of the semi I'd seen earlier from the balcony of the silo. I figured I'd try another way into the house, a back way through the loading dock but the last key slid in and with a twitch, the latch clicked free. I eased the door open a chink, just wide enough to see inside.

No sounds or signs of anyone around.

Ray had a key to unlock the Greenhouse doors, too. I wove my way through the rain forest keeping off the path and out of the footlights. Quickly my clothes became soaked from brushing against the misted leaves. When I reached Death's Door, there was no one in sight.

Then again, they could be inside the Porch.

There was only one way to find out. I punched in the long series of numbers Ray had me memorize.

Like magic, the door released.

"Here we go," I muttered to myself.

All was quiet inside. Still, there was a chance Tandre might be in there, down below, tuning up the magnets. Either way, I'd soon be seeing Lucia.

As I was about to enter the mudroom, I heard a rustle behind me. A dark shape crept out from a tree fern and I nearly jumped out of my skin.

Sylvia.

The girl shuffled toward me in a hooded raincoat and rubber duck boots.

"Where's Jean?" she asked, biting her lip.

"I don't know. Have you been waiting for him?"

"Where's Gudrun?"

The girl stared at me with hurt, unblinking eyes.

I shook my head. "Haven't seen her."

I'd forgotten about Gudrun, assuming she was also part of the plot.

"Where's Ray?"

"Don't know that either."

"Well, what are you doing here?" she demanded.

"I'll tell you. Inside."

Before shutting Death's Door behind us, I looked back to see who else might jump out. The only thing moving were drops of water dripping from leaf to leaf.

Sylvia glumly stared down the empty tunnel.

"So you don't know where Jean is?" I asked.

She pulled her hood down and shook her head.

"They locked me in my room," she said, her tousled hair hanging over one eye.

The girl's hardened demeanor was a far cry from the spirited, rambunctious little darling I'd seen before. And it occurred to me that she knew things she didn't want to know.

"You got hurt." She pointed at my face.

"Oh, that. Yeah, got banged up a bit."

I must've been quite a sight. Black and blue nose, swollen lip, clothes soaked to my skin.

An agonized cry made both of us cringe. Then, *Zt!* The Leaker was silenced.

"So, you were saying… they locked you in your room?"

"They do that sometimes," she said. "But I can get out. Gudrun said she'd come for me and we'd go on an adventure. But I couldn't wait. I went looking for her. Only I got scared this time." Sylvia's fingers curled into little fists. "Things are all changed around. What are they doing to my house?"

Zt!

What could I say? Tell her what I knew about Roe and his dead mother's takeover? Tell her Tandre's silo was burning up in flames? That she's being sent off to some school and probably not see her father for a long time, if ever? No, that wasn't going to come from me. Instead, I tried calming her down, explaining how they redecorated the house to show it off to some people who were looking to invest money in the place.

She folded her arms across her belly.

"They're sending me away to some school."

"Did they tell you that?"

"I just know."

She looked at me with sharpened eyes.

"It's true, isn't it?"

I didn't have a helpful answer for that. Never had any firsthand experience relating to kids, especially such a scrappy, precocious, and shaken little girl who communes with the dead.

"I'm going to talk to my Daddy."

"Okay," I said.

"I see him everyday. But they said not today. I asked them why and they didn't tell me."

"Well, you can talk to him now. Let's go, but keep your boots on."

She led the way.

"Who hurt you?" she asked as we crawled out of the tunnel.

So I shared with her how they tried to throw me out. I told her about Lucia, and Lucia's death. I pulled the crotal bell out of my pants pocket and held it out for her to see.

"Lucia gave this to me many years ago. It's what started me making bells."

Sylvia took the little bell out of my hand and jiggled it.

"The only reason I came back was to see her," I said. "If only for a minute. Then I'll take my bell and go."

"We'll have to ask my Daddy first," she said.

"Of course," I reluctantly agreed.

She pulled a tuning fork out of the pocket of her raincoat and handed it to me.

"Here's your thing back."

"Wow, thanks." I'd forgotten about it.

I stuck the fork in my back pocket and followed her up the ramp onto the deck. She went straight to the podium and called for Caspian.

Nothing happened.

She called again, louder.

The cloud shimmied from the sound waves of her voice. Nothing more.

"Where's my Daddy?"

"We had some trouble earlier," I said.

"What trouble? What's going on? What did they do to my Daddy?!"

Zt!

I had a hunch their takeover had already begun and Roe's mother was restricting access from the other side. But I kept it to myself. Still, if Sylvia couldn't reach her father, what chance did I have of contacting Lucia? So, I decided to go under the Porch floor and see if I could jar things loose by giving the bell a bong. I didn't get two steps when we heard the whoosh of Death's Door and the murmur of voices in the distance.

Sylvia and I went over to the lip of the deck and peered down the tunnel.

"Are you ready to see the ultimate wonder of the world?"

It was Roe with the three people I'd seen earlier in the conference room.

"Go on in," Roe said. "You'll find coat racks inside."

We watched the guests enter the mudroom and remove their shoes.

"Who's that with Uncle Len?" Sylvia said.

"He's your uncle?"

Zt!

"No, I just call him that. He's really my half-brother."

Half-brother, right, of course.

"Listen to me," I said, moving toward the ramp. "We should get off the deck. If they find us here…"

Sylvia wasn't listening, or budging. I tried another approach.

"Hey, you want to hear a secret?"

"What?"

That got her attention.

"I can't tell you here. I don't want them to hear it. Come on."

She followed me down the ramp only to stop partway to spy on the people in the mudroom.

"Hurry up," I whispered.

Sylvia trailed behind me as I made my way in the dark down to the orchestra pit. Seeing how easily she descended the steep stairs it was obvious she'd taken them before.

"Who are those people?" she asked.

"The investors I told you about."

"I don't like how they feel to me. Why isn't Jean here with them?"

"Shh." I pulled Sylvia aside. "We need to be quiet. If they find out I'm here they'll throw me off the property and I'll never see Lucia."

Pretty selfish of me considering Sylvia's world was crumbling to ruins around her.

"So, what's the secret?"

"Hang on."

From where we stood we couldn't see Roe's guests crawl through the long tunnel. We could only hear their intermittent grunts and mutterings of irritation.

"Yes, the knees get a workout," Roe said. "But it's all worth it as you shall soon see."

"Nothing's going to bite me, right?" One of the men

said.

"You're perfectly safe."

"It's wet in here," the man went on.

"Did you say wet?" Roe echoed down the tunnel. The last to enter.

Uh-oh. That's from Sylvia and me.

"I still don't know why I'm here," the woman said. "I mean, I know why Hiram's here, he's loaded. "What about you, Samuel?"

"What about me?"

One by one they crawled out of the tunnel and stood up on their feet. Roe came out last. He leaned on his cane to brace his robotic legs as he labored to stand himself upright. His face appeared tense. I knew he couldn't see us in the darkness of the orchestra pit, but the tightness of his jaw and how he fidgeted with the knob of his cane were clear signals of either anxiety or some troubling nuisance cramping his style. He knew someone in wet clothes had been here.

He tapped his cane on the floor a couple times before addressing his guests.

"Welcome to the most extraordinary structure on Earth. More breathtaking than the Sistine Chapel, Chartres Cathedral and the Taj Mahal combined."

The faces of the guests looked a bit lost, scanning around the lofty space as their eyes adjusted to the darkness.

"Believe it or not, you are now standing inside a structure designed for you to see and speak directly to departed souls."

Roe slowly ascended the spiral ramp to the Porch

deck.

"Follow me, please. Watch the foot lights."

"Psst…" I beckoned Sylvia through the opening that led down under the Porch floor.

As we made our way down the ramp, she saw the distant spotlights shining on the bell below.

"What's your bell doing down there?"

"Shh… Jean's idea. And your Father's. We rang it earlier and angels came."

"Can I hit it?"

"No."

"So what's the secret you're going to tell me?"

"Wait."

"No, I'm not going to wait."

"Shhh… please. "

We stopped midway down the ramp and listened to Roe talking to the men.

"… like having a video conference call with the dead," he said. "Sound preposterous? Absolutely. But what if it were true? Think about it for a moment. And think what it would mean if you owned a stake in such a phenomenon. A financial stake in the one and only portal that leads to the secrets of the Afterlife, or what I fondly refer to as the Immortal Portal."

"Which goes to my question again. Why me?" the woman asked. "You said we were hand-picked. But I'm in no position to invest in anything."

"Ah, but you bring something every bit as valuable, Josie," Roe replied. "Which you shall soon understand."

Sylvia grasped me by the forearm. "I know your secret. You know why I can't see my Daddy, don't you?"

"Maybe," I said. I wasn't going to lie to her. I knew what was coming. Roe's mother was about to make her grand entrance. Just the thought of the dead woman made me want to wretch.

"It's because of them, isn't it," Sylvia said.

"Shh... you'll soon find out."

There. I told her without telling her. Me and my big mouth.

Zt!

A Nansa appeared in the doorway at the top of the ramp.

"Ahh, there's one there!" Sylvia pointed to it with a smile on her face that quickly faded when the Nansa vanished.

"Now," Roe said. "I will ask you all to turn your attention to the misty egg floating in the center of the space and watch what happens when I address it."

In the corner of my eye I spotted another Nansa down in the depths, hovering beside the bell. When I looked back to tell Sylvia, she was gone. So much for agreements with a seven-year old.

"Angelina," Roe's voice deepened in pitch. "I call for Angelina."

Who's Angelina?

I tiptoed up the ramp looking for the girl and found her back on the landing of the orchestra pit. Her eyes transfixed on the face shaping itself out of the cloud.

The silvery face of Roe's mother.

"Greetings, Leonard," Angelina said through a serene smile.

The guests shuffled and squirmed, firmly clutching onto their disbelief.

"Hello Angelina." Roe grinned. "I brought along some new friends. Allow me to introduce you to Josie Tremont. This is Samuel Lenger. And this is Hiram Zetz."

"Hello and a warm welcome to each of you. I am Angelina, your guide to the Afterlife."

Sylvia looked back at me and gave a sour face. I pressed a finger to my lips.

"Okay, this is truly weird," Josie said.

"That it is," Roe replied. "As well as truly real. We have done it. We've finally made visual and audible contact with those on the other side."

"Is there someone you wish to speak to?" Roe's mother asked. "A loved one or relative who has passed on?"

Her voice sounded smoother, creamier than when I heard her speak earlier. All the more sickening.

The guests didn't readily answer.

"Mr. Lenger," Angelina said.

"That's me," Samuel answered.

"You have a grandfather on your mother's side, do you not?"

"Don't we all?" Samuel's tone was curt.

"Allow me to explain," Roe turned to Samuel. "The reason Angelina inquires about family is because the instrument most effectively materializes those in one's bloodline as well as intimate relations who've passed away."

"His name is Barth, I believe," Angelina said.

"How'd you know that?"

"Would you like to speak with him?"

"No, I would not," the man said.

Roe lifted his hands beseechingly. "But how else are you to see that this miraculous instrument delivers on its promise?"

"I said no. I will not speak to him."

"Who was he?" Josie asked.

"A vicious industrialist who worked behind the scenes manipulating the decisions of governments on how to capitalize on war."

"So that's it!" Josie shot up. "It's our blood lines. We've been selected because we're all descendants of power brokers."

"Very astute, Josie," Roe said.

"So then I guess you want me to contact my great grandfather, right?" Josie asked.

"Who's that?" Hiram Zetz asked.

"Well, the family rumor maintains he was a member of some secret, elite fraternity, and stashed away a ton of ill-gotten gold bullion somewhere."

"Sounds a lot like my grandfather." Hiram swung around to Roe. "Is this the reason you flew us all here? To dredge up the ghosts of our accursed ancestors."

Roe didn't flinch. He merely shifted his weight from one leg to the other before answering.

"It's one of our research studies. Since we now can contact the dead, we can learn the truth about the past— who was who, and if they really were who we believe. But we need close relations to connect with them. And, concurrently, we're also seeking investors to help fund more instruments like this."

"It all sounds very intriguing, but its horseshit."

Roe stiffened. "How do you mean, Josie?"

"I mean there's no secret society or stockpile of buried gold in my family. All these occult assertions about elite fraternities and shadow governments masterminding world affairs. It's a crock perpetrated by paranoid conspiracy junkies."

"No, it's not," Hiram said. "The Dark Fathers were quite real."

"What was his name, Ms Tremont?" Angelina asked.

"Who, my great grandfather?"

"Yes."

"Oh, well evidently he went by a couple names. One was Hayden."

"I'm sorry, could you repeat that name," Angelina requested.

"I said his name was Hayden Krall," Josie shouted, not knowing she was calling the man out of the dead.

Roe ushered Josie closer to the podium and urged her to repeat the name.

"Hayden Krall."

Roe smiled and turned to the cloud as Angelina evaporated, only to be replaced by the stern face of a man who looked about, disoriented.

Hayden Krall, no doubt.

But as abruptly as his face appeared, Roe stepped to the podium.

"Angelina," he called his mother back.

They'd gotten what they wanted. The cloud registered Krall's sonic signature for them to access anytime.

"And you, Samuel," Angelina continued.

My stomach leaped into my throat.

Shit! They're going after the evil titans of old. That's the alliance Roe's mother mentioned. But why? Besides the money, why would they want access to them?

A shadow whisked past me. It was Sylvia.

Oh God, the girl's going to blow it.

She stomped up the stairs of the orchestra pit onto the Porch ramp.

"Who are you!" she shouted at Angelina.

Roe swiveled at the podium nearly tripping over his legs.

"I am Angelina. Leonard?"

Roe squinted into the dark recesses and spotted the girl.

"What are you doing here?"

"Where's my Dad?" the girl demanded.

"Excuse me." Roe turned from his guests.

"What is it?" His mother demanded. "Leonard?"

"It's Sylvia. I'll be right back."

"Leonard, you said she wouldn't be here."

"You can't stop me from seeing my Daddy."

"My dear." Roe gingerly stepped to the edge of the deck. "No one's stopping you from seeing your Daddy. Where did you get such an idea?"

"Who's that woman?"

"This is private, Sylvia. Now, how did you get in here? Is Gudrun with you?"

"I called for my Dad, but he didn't come."

"Gudrun!" Roe called out.

"And you're going to send me away to some school, but you never asked me, and…" Sylvia's voice cracked, "…and then I won't ever see my Daddy."

"Where did you hear such nonsense?"

"From that man." She pointed toward me in the dark of the orchestra pit.

That's it. It's all over for me now.

"What man? Where? Sweetie, this is not the time," Roe strained to sound calm and kind. "I told you we were having some very special guests."

"No you didn't."

"The little girl is the daughter of Charles Caspian," Angelina said, attempting to pacify the guests.

"Well, yes, I did tell you," Roe said to the girl. "But you may not have heard me."

Sylvia stopped listening to him and zoned in on his mother.

"She talks like she knows me."

"Yes, well dear, everybody knows you." Roe tried to reach for Sylvia's arm with his hand, but he was too tall.

"I want to talk to my Daddy, now."

"And soon you shall." Roe nudged Sylvia with his cane. "But we need to get you back to your room so that our guests… "

Sylvia slapped at Roe's cane. "Stop poking me!"

Roe snarled, "You self-entitled little… if you don't mind me this minute you will not see your Daddy for a long, long time."

Roe kept prodding her down the ramp toward the mouth of the tunnel. But she dodged his cane and jumped away.

"You come back here!"

"Leonard!" Angelina barked.

"Hold on, please." Agitated, Roe headed to an intercom mounted on the wall next to the tunnel and paged security.

Everything was shaking loose and the impulse to blow Roe's conspiracy to pieces was unstoppable.

To hell with it. If Roe and his mother seize control I'll never see Lucia anyway.

I stumbled down the ramp under the Porch and crossed the hard rock floor to the inner circle of magnets where the bell hung.

Two Nansa zipped past me, eating Leakers.

I picked the mallet off the floor, reared back and slammed the bell full force.

BWOHHH-WOO-WAH-ONGGG!

The ear-shaking strike tone lifted me off the floor, stripping the mallet right out of my hands. I covered my ears as a torrent of magnetic energy flooded my body.

Deafened by the toll, but dying to see what was happening, I hustled back up the ramp. Adrenalin's a great painkiller. And so are ultrasonic magnetic waves.

When I reached the orchestra pit the entire Porch had lit up like a luminous fountain. Angelina's face was faint. She was chattering a blue streak but my ears were ringing so loud I couldn't make out a word she was saying. The guests stood like stone statues, utterly mesmerized. Sylvia was beaming. Her glazed eyes dazzling in the swarm of lights. Next to her on the ramp, Roe looked on, cadaver-white, watching his mother's face wobble like gelatin.

Gradually, the bell tones subsided and my hearing returned.

"Wee!" Sylvia cheered.

"My God. That was amazing!" Josie shouted.

"What is that sound!" Angelina warbled. Her face stretched out of proportion.

"It's the bell!" Sylvia chimed.

"Show that again!" Hiram insisted.

"A bell?" Angelina sounded appalled.

"Yes, a bell," Roe shouted back in rage.

"Well stop it right now!"

"No, ring it again, please," Samuel requested. "That was quite marvelous."

"Where is it?!" Roe leaned over into Sylvia's face, steadying himself with his cane. "Where's the bell!"

I didn't wait to hear her tell him. I rushed back down the ramp under the cloud floor. This time I tore two pieces off the Past-Pastor's paper note, wadded them into little balls and stuffed them in my ears. I gripped the mallet handle tight as I could, locked my legs and walloped the bell in two successive strokes.

BWOHHHONGGG!

The first hit sent me sprawling to the floor, my arms convulsing from the mallet head quaking in my hands. I didn't wait for the peal to play out. I scrambled to my feet and struck the bowl of the bell a second time.

BWOHHHONGGG!

Again the magnetic surge forced me backward. Gathering my wits, I hoofed it up the ramp. And there, to my delight, Angelina's face began twisting into hideous contortions. Her voice became a hissing shrill and moments later her silver image blew away in a blizzard of glorious rays.

"Ha!" I laughed out loud.

Up on the deck, Roe's guests stood enraptured. Streaks of tears shone on Hiram's cheeks.

High overhead diamond lenses of star-bright light spread in a widening arc mirroring the shape of the dome ceiling, creating a giant, dazzling hemisphere. And from below, with a drumming thunder, a rose-shaped light-form sprung from under the cloud. Up it came in earthy colors, swelling around us— a second hemisphere rising to meet the one above.

Around the center, a band of Nansa interlaced string-like rays between the upper and lower domes, feverishly working to join them into one complete sphere.

The united state— where the spiritual and physical worlds fuse as one. A reality that's always been here. Untouched, unseen, unknown. We simply hadn't found a way to reach its rarefied home.

Go find Roe, I urged myself.

I climbed the stairs out of the orchestra pit, certain the spectacle would wake Roe to his senses.

He found me first.

"You, you son of a bitch!"

He speared the silver tip of his cane into my Adam's apple, pressing me back against the wall next to the tunnel.

Look, it's almost complete," I gulped, latching

onto his cane with my hands. "Let me ring it one more time!"

"No!" he roared, jabbing the needle-sharp point of the cane until it pierced the skin of my throat. "You move an inch, I'll puncture your vocal chords and you'll never speak again!"

What's with this guy? Doesn't he see what's happening?

The percolating bell tones quieted down. The lights receded. I released my grip on the cane and lowered my hands in surrender.

"Forgive the disruption, gentlemen," Roe called out to his guests. "For every miracle there's a rat. We will resume our demonstration once security extracts this one."

A dribble of blood oozed out my neck and trickled down my chest. I felt fastened to the spot, unable to move a muscle.

The guests chattered on ecstatically.

Roe ignored them.

"How did you get in here? Did Gudrun let you in? Just nod. Did Gudrun put you up to this?"

A smile cracked my face at the thought of Gudrun posing another threat to Roe's plot. I didn't nod or shake my head. I just sucked air into my nostrils. I knew it was only a matter of time before Gorno and Julian would show up. And I wasn't going to let that happen. Better to risk a perforated windpipe than be pulverized and have that old bullet in my chest pop an artery.

Lucky for me, out of the blue...

BWOHONGGG!

The bell! She did it! The rascal rang the bell!

Stunned by the sound and sudden burst of light, Roe's cane flexed enough for me to jerk my head free, drop to the floor and scuttle into the tunnel.

Roe came after me, whacking me with his cane as he teetered, dropped to his knees and entered the tunnel. I kicked the cane away, but he kept coming at me.

"Sylvia, hit it again!" I shouted, though I knew she couldn't hear me with her ears still ringing from the first strike.

"Do you realize what you're doing?" Roe blurted, murder in his eyes.

"Calling the angels," I said.

"Angels? These guests are the angels! They're the money. And without them we lose it all!"

Reaching the mudroom, I hunkered down and screamed back at him. "Look man! Are you blind?"

I pointed at the brilliance behind him.

Roe glanced back as a current of ultrasonic light came gushing up the tunnel like a blast of water from a fire hose.

"Higher souls!" I whooped, holding my throat.

A surge of brilliant light swept into the mudroom stippled with tiny golden pearls that tingled the bell tones against my skin. It felt like my body had become a pipe organ and the pearls were striking chords deep inside my very being.

Roe struggled to his feet, slack-jawed, dumbstruck. He wiped a hand across his forehead, his unblinking eyes mesmerized by the beads of light darting and flashing around his head like fireflies. And there, for one fleeting moment, all hatred of the man drained off me.   I felt only compassion for the maimed and abandoned child inside him, and for his mother's torment, and the score she felt compelled to settle. I faced Roe elated and free of judgment. Giddily free. I never knew feeling good could feel that good.

"Surely you can hear them singing. You hear the lights." I could barely get the words out of my mouth.

Panting, Roe frisked me with a look of unexpected wonder and betrayal. His inner conflict so palpable I could hear his thoughts collide in his mind, 'This is not happening. Why are you doing this to me? I can't let this change anything.'

And yet he couldn't deny the inescapable— the pearls of light kissing his face.

"Let it go, man. You're free now," I said.

Roe's lips quivered, his eyelids twinkled with tears. I knew he'd reached a turning point in his mind, and his life.

"It's not yours or your mother's," I went on. "This belongs to the light beings. They're what it's all about. This is why Caspian wants the bell here."

Instantly Roe's face burned cold.

A fateful mistake. I should never have called his father's name. It appears Roe's pain is greater than his heaven.

The red button on the mudroom wall lit up with alarm. Roe pounded it with an angry fist. A vacuum rush sounded. Death's Door swung open behind me and filling the threshold stood Gorno, huffing and puffing.

"Take him down!" Roe bellowed. "And where's Julian? We need the girl removed from here at once!"

Gorno took two steps inside the mudroom and stopped, so blinded by the lights he didn't see me standing in front of him. His mouth popped open as golden motes foamed over his big round head. The cue ball dropped from his hand and clacked on the limestone floor.

I ran free, trailing a cape of pearls behind me.

"What's wrong with you?" Roe raged. "Go! Go! He's getting away!" I heard Roe yell while I beat back ferns and vines.

Hearing the footfalls of others coming along the path I ducked under leaves and waited for them to pass. I felt cross-cut by conflicting emotions— defeated and saddened at not seeing Lucia, anxious about getting out of there, and at the same time filled with the euphoric freedom the light beings poured out.

But there was no going back.

The lobby was empty. Sparsely lit. The doors to the dining hall closed. Without hesitating I headed for the front door panting, sweat dripping in my eyes. Just as I took hold of the door handle a blue radiance flooded the glass floor under my feet.

Right behind me, filling the center of the lobby hovered a Nansa big as a whale.

"Holy shit," I gasped, banging back against the front door. And here I thought I'd seen everything.

At first the enormous being buoyed in mid-air like a balloon. Then it retreated a few feet as if to give my shock and amazement room to settle.

I'd been witness to some mind-boggling sights in the little time I'd been at the Sylvia House, but seeing this blue blimp of a spirit threw me into an altered state. Time stopped. I stared spellbound until my wits kicked in.

"They're taking control of it," I said. "I can't find the architect and I need to get out of here. So, you better do something or else that bridge you're building to unite the worlds is not going to happen."

There was no immediate response. The immense specter swayed hypnotically.

Surely I was in the presence of the Mother of all Nansa.

But I was wrong.

The Mother was actually a mass of them joined into one. As I soon found out when two Nansa peeled off the side of its body. They floated toward the wing of the south corridor and stopped. One flexed the upper half of its body toward the corridor while the lower half remained stationary.

"What? You showing me a better way out?"

Its feathery edges lit up.

"I take it that's a yes."

The Nansa uncoiled, then flexed its body again, beckoning me to follow it down the south corridor.

"What the hell." I waved it on. "Lead the way."

No sooner were the words out of my mouth when, like dandelion seeds blown into flight by a stroke of wind, the Mother Nansa disbanded in all directions at once.

"Slow down," I urged the two Nansa as I made my way down the corridor, stutter-stepping past doors with brass name plates on them: ADMINISTRATION, ELEVATOR, RESTROOMS, MAINTENANCE.

Zt!

The Nansa halted at the far end of the hallway in front of a red, EMERGENCY EXIT ONLY door. On the right wall, a door with the sign: SWIMMING POOL, SAUNA & WEIGHT ROOM. To the left, a blank steel door with no signage.

While one Nansa went about zapping Leakers, the other one drifted over to the non-descript door and flickered its outer tips three times.

"No, I have to get free of this place."

Again, it gave three flicks.

Whatever was inside that door, the Nansa seemed intent on me seeing it.

I pulled Ray's pouch of keys out of my shop coat, but realized the door handle didn't have a key slot. I spotted a security pad on the wall and punched in Ray's pass code for Death's Door.

It didn't work.

I tried again. Nothing. Either Ray never pirated its key code, or he didn't think it was important enough to be survival insurance.

"I don't know the pass code, and I need to get out of here." I said, glancing back and forth between the Nansa and down the long corridor to the lobby.

Nobody there. But I knew they'd be coming.

Zt! Zt!

A zapping frenzy started. The air around my ears

sizzled like a lightning storm as a Nansa munched Leakers non-stop. The other one slipped between me and the keypad, its outer fringe again pulsing three times.

Surely, it was trying to tell me something, but given my ragged state of mind and pain, I didn't catch the meaning straightaway. So it circled around, stopped at the keypad and blinked its tips three more times.

"What? Are you saying the first number in the code is three?" I punched the number 3 button on the pad. Then looked back at the Nansa. "There. Is that it?"

Its fringe pulsed five times. So I went ahead and pressed the 5 button. We repeated the process for the next number, and the next. Voices murmured in the distance. People in the lobby. I didn't bother to look. I just kept punching numbers until finally the door sprung free.

Inside, we entered a stark, olive green room lit by a couple bare ceiling bulbs in wire cages. I quickly pulled the door shut behind me and listened. All I could hear was a faint whirring, like from a mechanical fan. On the opposite wall was a large padded freight elevator with its door open.

The Nansa coaxed me inside.

"Okay, I'll play along, but this better be good."

The elevator panel had only two directional arrows— UP and DOWN.

"Which way?" I pointed my index finger at the UP button.

Not a blink.

I tapped the DOWN button. As the door slid closed

a gloom of dread seeped into my blood.

"I got a bad feeling about this. You?"

The Nansa didn't respond. But all of a sudden from the back corner of the elevator came an agonized shriek. Floating up off the floor was a Leaker, only this one had an eyeless face protruding from its dark mass with a lippy, fish mouth stretched wide and wailing.

The Nansa zapped it in a flash.

"Stay close," I told it. "Real close."

One floor down the elevator lurched to a stop. The door opened and a medicinal odor singed my nostrils. The same smell Gorno gave off.

We entered a narrow hallway at the end of which was another blank door with a security pad on the wall. Next to the steel door stood a rolling dumpster brimming over with pants, shirts, and shoes.

The Nansa and I repeated the drill with me tapping the sequence of numbers on the keypad that it signaled by flashing its tips.

The steel door opened onto a cinderblock room. A couple of soft amber wall sconces illuminated banks of computers and monitors displaying grids with numbers and wavy green and white lines.

What the hell is all this about?

All the tables and chairs were attached to wheels making me think the room was a rolling command center ready to be mobilized at the drop of a hat. I scanned the rows of knobs and dials. All techno-gibberish to me.

Maybe this is the reason they're so worried about Y2K.

Before I could ask, 'Why bring me down here?' the

Nansa slipped through a set of swinging double doors leading into a long rectangular space lined with privacy curtains that hung from horizontal stainless steel rods. It reminded me of a hospital ward at night, eerie and still, all except for a tinny, electronic whir coming from behind the curtains.

Curious, I parted one of the curtains and found a man lying on a hospital bed, a white sheet up to his neck. His body was motionless. Eyes shut. Clear tubes snaking down under the bed.

What is this place?

My first impression was they'd set up some kind of research laboratory where they studied the dying. I pulled back the next curtain and found another rigid, unconscious body.

The Nansa beckoned me around the far corner to an adjoining room with even more curtains and beds. A low-pitched motor groaned somewhere off in the distance. I approached the cubicle where the Nansa now floated. I slid the curtain aside and there on the bed was the body of Jean Tandre. His eyes half-closed. His face puffy, blank, bloodless.

The sight staggered me. Such a flamboyant personality lying lifeless as a rolled-up rug. I lifted the sheet. Electrode leads had been attached to his shaved chest and plastic tubes injected into each forearm. Under the bed was a rack of digital monitors and machines I assumed measured heart rate and other vital signs. I leaned my ear to his heart and heard it thump like a limp bass drum.

"Wake up." I shook his body. "Come on, snap out

of it."

But it was like pushing on a flat tire.

As I stared in disbelief I recalled Gorno say, "Last I saw he was napping."

Napping, hell, he's in a coma. They intentionally put all these people into comas.

I straightened up and took in the entire ghoulish scene— bed after bed of people suspended between life and death.

But why?

I turned to the Nansa. "Do you know what's happening here?"

Then the obvious hit me like a brick. Of course, in their own way each one of these people endangered Roe's precious plan. Or at least he suspected they might. He couldn't have them alive or dead. If he killed them, they could still talk. Their spirit could show up on the Porch and name their murderer, like Janie did. Far better to have them undead, locked away in some speechless netherworld.

I recalled Roe using the name, 'Limbo Room,' when he was talking to Dora, the nurse.

This is the place he was talking about.

"What are they planning to do with these people?" I asked the Nansa. "And who the hell is minding the store?"

It seemed morbidly neglectful to be sustaining all these comatose bodies with no one around checking on them.

Then I remembered Ray in his drunken outburst say, "Poof! People disappear around here."

You got that right.

There was no doubt in my mind Ray was down there, tucked under some sheet with intravenous tubes jammed into his wily veins. He of all people knew something was up. So much for getting back at them with his posse comitatus.

But surely someone out in the world, some friend or relative is searching for these people.

I crossed the aisle, flung back another curtain to find the saddest face I'd ever seen— Sarah, the Past-Pastor's daughter, flat on her back, the gleam of a tear hanging in the corner of her right eye.

Well, the Past-Pastor knows she's missing.

Turning back to the Nansa, I threw up my arms.

"So tell me, why would you ever want to knit your world with ours? I mean just look around. This sort of savagery we do in the name of power and greed is only going to contaminate yours."

It didn't flicker.

Repulsed, I closed the curtain and stepped into the aisle at a loss at what to do. I couldn't detach all the feeding tubes and watch the people wake up and walk out of there. Whatever fluids being dispensed were sustaining their bodies. If I disengaged the tubes I could jeopardize their lives.

"Okay, I've seen enough." I said out loud. "I better get out of here and report this to the police before they stick me under a sheet."

That's when I realized that this was where Gorno intended to take me. "Change of plans," he'd said. "You're going back to the house. "To get my bell?" I'd asked. "Yeah, to get your bell rung."

Just then, the Nansa flew at my face and froze an inch from my nose, its tips flashing with alarm.

"What now?"

WHOP-WHOP!

That can only be the sound of the double doors swinging open.

The fluorescent ceiling lights pulsed on.

Someone's coming!

I sidestepped into the nearest bed and carefully pulled the curtain shut. The body on the bed was April, the irate woman who had accused Tandre of committing a holy crime. No surprise there.

My whole body tensed up as a dark shape marched past me. I peered through a slit and saw the stocky frame of Dora, standing at the far wall holding a piece of rolling luggage by her side. A loud crunk! shook the air followed by a rattling grate as a loading dock door lifted on its track.

Brash yellow light poured into the room.

Outside an engine idled. A hunched figure stood on the dock trailing coils of cigarette smoke.

"There you are," the man said. "I been waiting an over an hour."

His accent sounded familiar.

The banquet. The Russian who sat next to me.

Zt!

"Take this," Dora said, handing him her luggage and a manila envelope. "Tell me you have the maps and contact details?"

"Packed in the cab." The cigarette dropped from the

man's fingers. Sparks bounced off the dock. "Ready when you are," he said as he scuffed out the butt and took her luggage.

"Check all the instruments. I'll start bringing them out one at a time."

"I checked them."

"Then check them again, Vadim."

The woman came back inside, strapping a surgeon's mask over her face as she walked.

Through the gap in the curtain I saw portable halogen work lights illuminating the dock area. I could also see the back of a semi-trailer parked up against the dock. A translucent screening fabric had been rigged to poles hung between the rear wall of the house and the roof of the semi-trailer. The same truck I'd seen earlier from the silo with Tandre's binoculars.

"Dora," the man called out, "Still nine?"

The woman stopped in the aisle two feet from me and lifted her mask.

"No, ten now," she said, then continued on around the corner into the adjacent room.

"Ten." The Russian raised the rear retractable door of the trailer.

What are they doing, transporting the bodies somewhere else? Is that why they hung those screens on the dock— to cloak their vanishing act?

Rows of ceiling lights softly illuminated the trailer's interior. All I could make out were shelves with cords hanging down. The curtain I hid behind obscured the rest.

Seconds later I felt the shimmying tremor of wheels

on the floor. It was Dora, pushing one of the rolling beds out onto the dock and into the back of the trailer. More sounds followed— the muttering of their voices in the trailer and a series of mechanical snaps. My guess, they were securing the bed inside the trailer to some sort of apparatus.

So far, I counted only Dora and the Russian, Vadim. I figured he was the truck driver, she the nurse. I didn't know if there were any others outside, on the dock or in the truck.

Hell, this could be just one in a number of shipments. For all I know there may be a facility somewhere packed with tiers of comatose bodies.

The urge to mess up their madness boiled up in me like an unstoppable force. These people had gone too far. I couldn't detach myself anymore.

This *was* my fight.

As I reached into my back pocket for the tuning fork Sylvia had given back to me, I heard the whop-whop sound of the double doors again.

"Dora?" A voice called out as footsteps rounded the corner.

"Where have you been?" Dora shouted from the dock. "We're behind schedule."

"Got delayed."

It was Julian, coming down the aisle with Sylvia asleep in his arms.

Seeing the girl, Dora stormed up to Julian and stuck a stiff hand in his face to stop. "Don't you bring her down here!"

"Relax, she's sedated," he said. "But we need to get

her hooked up and in the truck."

"What? You're joking. Not Sylvia." Dora didn't believe him.

"Yes. Sylvia. In the truck."

"No, no, the girl is to be sent away to school."

"Change of plans," Julian said.

"Oh my God. Leonard ordered this?"

"Zero risk. No loose ends."

"But we're full up."

"Now hear this— Sylvia goes. Make room."

Dora bit her lip, obviously upset about Sylvia. "What about Gudrun?" she asked.

"Not a clue. Still can't find that woman," Julian said. A tinge of panic in his voice.

Dora swept back a curtain. "Well, set the girl down here for now and help me get these beds in the trailer."

Julian laid the girl on an empty bed across the aisle from me.

Zt! Zt!

Leakers were getting zapped rapid-fire. Julian and Dora didn't appear to notice any of it as they went back to the adjacent room.

"Wash your hands first," Dora said. "I'll get you a mask. Then I'll show you how to disengage the beds properly."

"I don't need a mask."

"It's not for you, it's for them."

"Fuck'em," Julian said.

Sylvia was lying on her side across the aisle. Her mouth slightly open. A bubble of drool between her lips. I felt the bite of guilt for leaving her back at the

Porch. Afterall, she rang the bell that freed me from the prick of Roe's cane. Now these monsters were going to put her out. They had to. She knew too much, talked too much, and sending her away to some private school in London was not going to cut it.

"Vadim will show you where to position the beds in the truck," Dora called back to Julian as she pushed another bed past me.

"So where is he?" Julian's footsteps came marching toward the curtain I hid behind.

Dora shouted something from inside the trailer. I raised the tuning fork in my fist like a dagger.

Curtains burst open in the next bed.

"There you are, heh-heh-heh," Julian snickered at Tandre's bedside. "What's wrong, Jean? You don't look so good."

Julian jostled with the bed, trying to maneuver it out into the aisle.

"Be careful with the feeding tubes!" Dora scolded him. "What did I tell you!"

"Got it," Julian said, grappling with something before rolling Tandre's bed away. "Au revoir, Johnnie God."

Now I'm thinking it's only a matter of time before they come to April's bed where I am.

Then what? Defend myself with a tuning fork?

I waited for Dora to go around the corner into the next room. When she did, I rushed across the aisle, lifted Sylvia's limp body over my shoulder and grabbed a folded sheet off the bed.

"Hey, this is the architect." Vadim stopped the bed

at the tailgate.

"Yeah," Julian said. "What of it?"

I could see Julian step up to Vadim in the trailer, which was teched-out like a mobile ICU.

"We're taking him out?" Vadim sounded stunned.

"You got a problem with that?" Julian said.

"I didn't know he was…" Vadim abruptly stopped.

"You're not getting paid to know. Your job is to drive the truck and keep your Russian mouth locked shut."

With the two pre-occupied in the trailer, I made a dash for the dock carrying the girl, only to trip on a power cord. One of the light stands jiggled for a second. I swift-kicked the cord off my foot and slipped out through a gap in the screen.

A light drizzle patted my head as I bare-footed down the concrete steps onto the rear driveway, the wet gravel stinging like thumb tacks. Reaching the stone wall of the Porch dome I turned around and looked back. No sign of Gorno or any guards. Sylvia moaned in my arms, delirious.

"It's okay, it's me, the bellmaker," I whispered as I made my way along the Porch wall to a tree next to the driveway. I lowered the girl onto the ground. Her body squirmed and jingled.

"Took a lot of guts for you to ring the bell."

Sylvia couldn't hear a word, but I said it anyway.

"Gudrun was right. You're one feisty troublemaker."

Her eyeballs rolled under the lids. She smacked her lips.

Good. She'll soon be coming to.

I stuck some fallen branches in the dirt around her

body and set the sheet over them making a tent cover to keep out the rain.

Two Nansa followed us and drifted next to Sylvia's side.

"We got to get her out of here to a safe place," I told them.

My thoughts were racing. I knew that any minute they'd find her missing and come beating the bushes looking for her. The one and only plan that came to mind was to take the girl to the Past-Pastor's place in Newgrange. But not just yet. I couldn't live with myself if I didn't first try to stop that truck before it drove off in the night.

"Will you stay with her?" I asked the Nansa, and lurching forward, I dug my bare heels in the earth and stood my body up. "Time to shake up this horror show."

I slunk along the tree line and hunkered behind a pile of scaffolding looking to see who else might be around. Wiffs of steam rose off the hood of the truck. I looked in the cab. Nobody there. I crossed the driveway on the balls of my feet, unlatched the driver side door of the truck and climbed in.

As my hands fumbled around under the steering wheel, I heard the whizzing jet of an air vent behind my head and muted voices talking inside the trailer. Finally my fingers tingled the keys. I yanked them out, killing the engine.

"Hey!" Someone reacted from the dock.

Shoving the door open with my foot, I slid off the seat and dropped to the driveway.

"We lost power!" Vadim shouted.

Then everyone started yelling at once. I shuffled away, grimacing with every step. I'm halfway back to the tree where I left Sylvia when the air shook with a gun shot.

My whole body bristled.

"One more step and you're going down!"

It was Julian.

My shoulders slumped. I turned and faced him.

"Going for a ride, Julian?"

"You, you speck of shit!" He stood twenty feet from me, the barrel of his weapon leveled at my chest. "You got one doozie of a death wish coming back here."

"Julian!" Dora hollered from the dock. "What's happening?"

"Just finish loading the trailer!"

"Yeah, Julian, what's happening?" I said. "What are you going to do with all those people, huh?"

"You're about to find out, you fuck. But first things first. Toss me the keys."

"Don't do this, man. Don't be a fool. Roe's planning to do the same thing with you. What, do you think you're indispensable? You're nobody. Squat."

"Wake up, Ding Dong. The longer you hold those keys the longer the life support system in that truck is down. That puts their life in your hands. They're all about to flat-line any minute now, and you'll be their executioner."

That gave me pause. But I wasn't going to give in just yet.

"No, you wake up. You're going to be on that next

truckload if you don't stop this insanity."

Julian wasn't buying it.

A screech chilled my bones. It came from the metal legs of a work light Vadim scraped across the dock to light the interior of the trailer.

CRACK!

Another gunshot clapped the air. It sounded like someone had kicked in a door. The bullet snapped a branch in the woods close to where Sylvia slept.

Too close. My throat sucked in a ball of air.

"Now! The keys!" Julian demanded. "I'm getting wet. And I hate getting wet."

"You mean these?" I jangled the truck keys in my outstretched hand, stalling for a miracle. A snowflake in hell.

"Julian!" It was Dora. "Where's Sylvia?"

"What?"

"She's gone!"

"Aw shit!" Julian punched the talk button on his walkie-talkie. "Big G. Hey Gorno! Pick up!"

"We're almost loaded!" Vadim shouted and started pulling down the screening fabric on the dock.

"Don't shut the trailer yet!" Julian yelled back, clipping the walkie-talkie back on his belt and moving toward me. "Time's up. Those bodies are starting to pickle. If I don't have the keys in my hand..."

"You'll what? Kill me? I don't think so. I'll come back in that cloud on the Porch and tell everyone." I pointed at the truck. "Isn't that what this is all about?"

A flurry erupted behind me. Julian suddenly looked spooked. He back-peddled a couple steps as a white apparition came storming across the asphalt toward us, shrieking like a banshee.

What kind of ghost is this? I'm thinking, when I see two Nansa trailing after it.

Julian turned the gun at the white thing.

"No!" I flapped my hands in the air. "It's..."

Before I could say it, the white sheet lifted enough to reveal Sylvia stagger-stepping around, beating the sheet off her body and stumbling to her knees.

"Silly? God you scared the crap out of me." Julian exhaled a breath of relief and casually hid the handgun behind his back.

The girl struggled to her feet and looked around, groggy, rubbing her knees, trying to get her bearings.

"Dora, Sylvia's here!" Julian called out. "Come get her!"

"What are we doing?" Sylvia yawned and wiped the drizzle from her drowsy eyes. "Where's Gudrun?"

The two Nansa came up beside her.

"Ah! Nansa! Do you see?" Sylvia took a couple clumsy steps toward the Nansa. It gave me an idea. I slipped my left hand into my shop coat pocket and unzipped Ray's pouch of house keys.

"Enough of the niceties." Julian whipped the gun out from behind his back. "Silly, come over here." He reached out and snatched the girl by her hair.

"Oww! That hurts!" Sylvia squealed.

"Dora!" Julian hollered.

"Okay, okay," I said. "You want the keys?"

Julian heard them jingle in my raised hand.

"Here, go fetch'em!" I heaved Ray's carabineer of

keys back over my head.

Julian's eyes rolled upward, following the flight of the keys into the darkness and drizzle.

They didn't reach the woods like I intended. They splashed off the dome roof of the Porch and slid to the ground.

"Vadim!"

Vadim didn't answer.

"God dammit." Julian shook his firearm in my face, "Don't you move!" He let go of Sylvia's hair and jogged past me to retrieve the keys.

I rushed to the girl and gave her a push.

"Come on, we're going to find Gudrun."

"He pulled my hair!"

"I know, I know. Now you need to run or he'll pull your hair again. Follow the Nansa. Fast as you can. Go!"

She didn't resist, but in her groggy state, all she could do was lope along. The two Nansa contorted their bodies, beckoning her to follow.

"Hurry up," I urged, taking hold of her left hand. "Fast as you can."

We made it as far as the front bumper of the truck when a gunshot rocked the air, and with it, a burning bite seized my left thigh. I cramped up, stumbled, and let go of Sylvia's hand. The girl felt me flounder. She hesitated for a moment but I waved her on.

"Go on! Follow the Nansa. They'll take you to Gudrun. I'll catch up."

But I didn't.

Julian and Vadim nabbed me before I could hobble

a few feet.

"Nice try, Ding Dong." Julian tore the truck keys from my fist and handed them to Vadim.

So much for shaking up their horror show.

Dora came hustling up.

"Help me get him in the truck," Julian ordered.

"What about Sylvia?" Dora asked.

"We'll deal with her later." Julian fingered Ray's keys in his hand. "My, my, look at all these. Don't tell me. Must be Freely's personal collection."

Vadim and Dora dragged me up the steps of the dock. The blood oozing from my bullet wound ran down my leg staining my foot red.

Julian pressed the walkie-talkie to his mouth.

"Gorno? Where the hell are you?"

Dora and Vadim leaned me up against the frame of the trailer door. Vadim hurried back down the steps to the driveway.

"Who is he?" Dora asked.

"He's poison. Go get the juice and let's get him rigged up."

"But he's shot."

"You can bandage him down the road. Now go, get the juice!"

The engine of the truck ignited. Its headlights came on.

"Back in business. Move it." Julian pushed me with the barrel of his gun across the tailgate and into the trailer.

With the interior lights illuminated, I could see the entire sterile crypt they'd created. White on white.

Pale-faced bodies tightly tucked under white sheets and harnessed to beds by white straps. Bed after bed bunched up against foam-sprayed walls with tanks mounted above them and clear plastic tube-like vines running into boxes with dials, buttons and more tubes. I was staring into the face of doom and it wasn't a world in ruins with charred corpses and smoking rubble. It was a white and sterile windowless room with rows of stiff, inoculated bodies covered like cocoons in white cotton. Only these cocoons would never become butterflies. They'd never become anything but a silent, roaring void.

As Julian pushed me past the beds with the point of his weapon, a question popped in my mind: If Roe and his mother were controlling who could and couldn't come through from the Afterlife, then why put me in a coma? Why not just kill me? If they can keep souls from showing up on the Porch and naming names, why not kill all these people?

Unless they fear someone else has their hands on the master plans. Someone who could build another Porch, another portal to the Afterlife. But who? Jean Tandre's in here.

I spun around on the balls of my feet and looked Julian dead in the eyes.

"Listen up, Julian. This is your last chance to smell the shit you're shoveling. You're going to be staring at prison walls for the rest of your life if you don't stop this madness right now."

"Prison? Heh-heh-heh." Julian let out his mocking laugh. "Don't you get it? I'll be so bitchin' rich I'll be unnn-touchable. Smelling the roses. We can talk more about what God-awesome wealth can buy when you're resuscitated. Right now we're in kind of hurry. Don't want to miss our connections."

Resuscitated, what a lie.

My old thorns were ripping out of my skin. I wasn't going down without a fight. I reached for the tuning fork in my back pocket on the verge of lunging at Julian's throat when I saw, emerging from the Limbo Room, none other than the beast himself.

Gorno.

"Finally! Lookie here, G-man, I got the one you let get away." Julian sounded victorious, boogie-stepping out of the trailer to greet the rhino.

Right off, I could tell there was something odd about the big man. How he strolled toward us with calm, almost graceful strides. His square shoulders now sloped at ease. His hands free of cue balls. His mean-slitted eyes looked soft under the work lights. No more the snorting rhino, the man stepping out onto the dock appeared blissfully at peace.

"Put the heater away," Gorno said.

"Sure." Julian lowered the weapon. "You can take over now while I round up Sylvia."

"Where'd she go?"

"Ran off. Not to worry. I'll get her."

"No, let her go," Gorno said. Then he looked inside the trailer at me. "Come on outta there, man."

Julian flinched. "No-no-no. This guy's an infection. He's like tetanus, man. He knows too much."

"We're not doing this, Julian." Gorno curled the fat

fingers of his right hand and waved me out of the trailer. "Come on out now."

Julian looked dumbfounded. "What are you talking about?"

I was dumbfounded too as I shuffled past the beds toward the dock.

"There's been a change," Gorno said, his bluster gone. "No more truck. We're bringing them all out. I'm in charge of this now."

"You crazy? There's no change." Julian looked beyond Gorno at the Limbo Room. "Dora!" he shouted.

As I edged toward the dock, I saw a gleam in Gorno's eyes. Pearls of gold twinkled in the bristle of his scalp.

The Porch, of course. Where else could that gleam come from? My God, Gorno saw the light beings.

Whatever he saw had transformed him.

Unreal.

I moved my bare feet onto the cold iron of the tailgate, inches from freedom. The madness of their gruesome plan was unraveling before me thanks to Gorno's startling intervention.

"Everybody freeze." Julian thrust his left hand at me in a halting gesture. "Nothing changes until I get confirmation."

He lifted the walkie-talkie to his ear.

"You saw them," I said, making eye contact with Gorno. "You saw the light beings."

The rhino's lips spread into a broad smile, and I wondered if Roe had a change of heart as well.

"You saw what?" Julian narrowed his eyes at Gorno.

"The Glory of God," Gorno uttered and knocked the walkie-talkie out of Julian's hand. It bounced off the edge of the dock and thumped on the ground.

"Hey!" Julian stiffened up. He pointed his pistol at the rhino. "What's gotten into you?"

The cab door slammed.

"I don't want to fight you," Gorno said in a friendly tone, "So, put your gun away like a good boy."

The Russian appeared in the driveway below the raised dock.

"Are we going?!" Vadim was pissed.

"A little help here. Gorno's gone wacko."

"We're running late!"

"Then do something fast!" Julian shouted.

A chaotic electricity crackled the air like anything could happen. All of it bad.

Panicked and squirrelly, Julian wiggled back away from Gorno and aimed the gun at my face. A vein sprouted from his forehead like a weld bead.

"You stay inside!"

Watch out, I told myself. Julian's losing it.

Gorno stepped between me and Julian.

"Not going to happen. So, drop it before somebody gets hurt."

"Too late for that," I said, gripping my thigh.

Julian pointed the gun back at Gorno's face.

"Back! Back the fuck away from me."

"What's going on here?" Dora emerged from the Limbo Room.

"About time you got here!" Julian shouted.

Dora held a syringe in one hand and a white cloth in

the other. No doubt soaked with chloroform or some other knockout narcotic.

Gorno didn't look at Dora or at me. His eyes were fastened on Julian. "I said drop it, now."

Gorno took a swipe at Julian's hand. He missed the gun but latched onto Julian's wrist and bent it backward. Julian grunted, twisted his torso and rammed his elbow into Gorno's teeth, flinching the rhino sideways a half step.

"Stop it you two!" Dora roared in vain.

They struggled, grappling for control of the weapon. A shot shattered the air. The bullet nicked the outer frame of the trailer and whisked past my ear.

Vadim jogged up the steps onto the dock wielding a length of steel scaffolding.

"Gorno, look out!" I hollered.

He didn't see it coming. Vadim whacked him on the side of his head with the bar. The gun flew free. Gorno shuddered from the blow and jostled to keep his feet. He gripped Julian's coat for support. They scuffled, punting the gun across the dock. It skidded off the side and under the truck.

Dodging the two men, I hopped down over the edge of the dock onto the driveway, relieved to be out of there.

Vadim cocked the steel bar high over his head, then dropped it like an axe on Gorno's skull. The big man's eyes popped up into his brain. His arms flopped to his sides and he fell face-first on the concrete.

"What have you done?" Dora howled at Vadim.

"He just saved our skins, that's what he's done,"

Julian said.

"Can we go now," Vadim said.

Julian kicked at Gorno's legs. "What got into you? Freak me fuckin' out!"

Vadim dropped the bar. It clanged on the driveway.

"I owe you one, man." Julian stuffed the gun into his shoulder holster, interlaced his fingers on top of his head and paced back and forth on the dock.

Standing in the shadows, I felt pulled to find Sylvia, but the chance of stopping the truck held me there.

Dora hunkered over Gorno and rolled him over on his back.

"He's still alive, but he's going to have one nuclear headache when he wakes up."

"He's not going to wake up," Julian said.

"What are you saying?"

"I'm saying he's meat gone bad. Pull out another bed. Stick that syringe in him and truck him out of here."

Dora glared at Julian. "You're going to have to explain this."

"I will! Just do it!"

Julian's walkie-talkie had landed a few feet away from the dock. I picked it up and limped around the other side of the truck searching the ground for his weapon.

"Where's that guy you shot? The guy who took the keys?" Dora asked, planting the syringe in Gorno's neck.

"I'll find him," Julian said. "Just get Gorno in there with the others and fix him up."

I looked under the truck. Behind the tires. No gun.

They dragged Gorno's body into the rig, and rolled in an empty bed.

Julian bellowed, "Okay, now go!"

"Catch that man!" Dora shouted at him.

"I'll handle it," Julian seethed. "Now get the hell out of here! I'll call you later."

The rear door of the trailer banged shut with Dora inside.

Vadim climbed into the cab and gunned the engine. A plume of black smoke spat out the exhaust. The truck rolled away, loaded with comatose bodies— Jean Tandre, Sarah, April. And now Gorno, my savior.

Unbelievable.

As the red taillights of the semi shrunk into the rainy night, I slumped out of the shadows and climbed the steps of the dock. Julian didn't see me hobble up behind him. He was sweeping the beam of a work light across the driveway, looking for his walkie-talkie and missing handgun.

Catching sight of something, he leaned over the edge just as I pounced on his back sending us both plunging off the dock onto the driveway in a heap. Halogen light stands toppled and crashed around us. Julian took the brunt of the fall. He tumbled over onto his back, stunned and groaning. I clambered on top of his chest, my knees digging into his shoulders. The tuning fork sprung out my back pocket and tinged on the ground.

"Call the truck back." I pressed the walkie-talkie to his lips.

He sneered and blinked back the rain.

"It's over, Julian. You're going to prison. It's just a question of how long. So turn that truck around right now."

He squirmed, kicked his legs, fighting to get free.

"No? Okay then." I grabbed one of the fallen light stands and held it in his face. "You know the saying, 'Go to the light'? Well this one's coming at you."

I didn't hesitate. I reared up and slammed the work light down hard, bashing his face with the business end. The halogen bulb burst. Blood spat in the air. Julian howled in pain.

"You were right, I'm not supposed to be here," I said. My body throbbed with animal ferocity. "But like my Grandpa says, "There's always a hitch.""

Julian's eyes sparked volts of hate at me.

I raised the light stand again and let out a gut-wrenching war cry.

"No!" He bucked his torso and wagged his hands around feebly attempting to block it.

"You going to call them?"

"You brog my node, muddafugga."

My arm stopped mid-strike.

"Broke it? I shattered your nasal bone. No smelling the roses now. Or ever. Call the truck back before I ram this into your mouth so hard you'll have to breathe through your asshole."

Julian's walkie-talkie squawked. I pressed the talk button.

"Yeah?"

"Jules, hey man, we got a break-in at the back gate! I can't reach Gorno! Call the others right away!"

"You need to call the truck back," I said to whoever was on the other end.

"What?"

"The semi. Call it back right now."

"What are you talking about? What semi? Julian? Who is this?"

"Who is this?"

"This is Speed. Who the hell are you?"

I shut off the unit.

A break in?

My first thought was the video camera at the back gate had caught me. But that couldn't be. I'd scaled the fence a hundred yards from the gate at least two hours earlier.

That's when I heard the belly-roar of a motorcycle.

Julian heard it, too. He heaved his body side to side, scooping up bits of gravel and flinging them at my face.

More rumblings sounded.

"Who's that?" I said, spotting a parade of headlights coming down the hill.

Julian craned his neck to see what was happening. I picked up the light stand.

"For the last time, call your truck back."

Julian looked back up at me. His eyes caught on something above my head.

"Fugg you." He smiled with bloody teeth and let out that cackle of his.

"You asked for it." I cocked my arm and froze.

"Drop it!" the voice commanded. It was the macho man who'd confronted me on the balcony of Tandre's silo. He stood above me on the dock, the cold nose of his rifle tapping against the skin of my neck.

"Relax, we just had a little disagreement." I lowered the work light down onto the driveway beside me. With my right hand I slyly latched onto the tuning fork that had popped out of my pocket next to my knee.

"Hands behind your head. Up... real slow-like. Do anything stupid, I blow you away. And I'm looking for a reason. So, please try something, I beg you."

I carefully cupped the tuning fork and exhaled a long, focused breath. *Go for the sweet spot,* I said under my breath, and wincing, I urged my legs to stand.

"What'd you say?"

"I said..." I swiveled and pitched the tuning fork at the man's head with all the strength I had left.

THNNG!

The fork struck him between the eyebrows. His rifle exploded with a jarring blast. He tipped backward and hit the concrete out cold.

I let out an aching groan, dropped my torso across the edge of the raised dock, my whole body shaking uncontrollably. Drenched to the bone. Utterly rung out. I didn't want to move, but the siren of a patrol car bolted me upright. There, racing down the hill, its red and blue lights flickered between the pine trees.

A welcome sight.

At my feet, Julian squatted on his knees among the fallen light stands, coughing blood and glomming onto the wreckage of his nose.

I leaned over him and snapped my fingers in his ears. "Now hear this," I said, and pointed toward the wail of the incoming siren.

I left Julian there and went searching for the girl.

"Sylvia!" I called out as I slipped and scratched my way up the rain-muddied slope around the south side of the house. She didn't respond. The thunder of a motorcycle roared back up the hill followed by the thumping of car doors and the murmur of people talking out front. Something was definitely afoot. Something at odds with Roe's plan.

Turning the corner I came upon a semi-circle of cars and trucks parked with their high beams spraying the house white. People stood alongside the vehicles in raincoats. I couldn't make out their faces at first, and when I did, I couldn't place them.

Limping closer I recognized the kind, turtle-headed cashier from the café in Newgrange and realized these people were locals. Behind their heads the red and blue emergency lights whirled from the roof of Sheriff Howard's patrol car.

"Hey! Whoa up there!" It was Speed racing across the garden, waving his arms at the townsfolk, his hoarse voice shouting, "You're trespassing here!"

They stared at him unmoved, unblinking. Nansa were hovering somewhere nearby, their bright blue radiance reflected in the drops of rain that pelted our faces with liquid light.

As I made my way toward the people, the front door swung open. Roe stepped from the threshold, two guards at his heels.

"They broke through the southern gate!" Speed explained to him. "I couldn't stop them!"

Roe wagged a hand at Speed to relax. He put on a meet-and-greet smile, and strode toward the uninvited visitors, cane in hand, making it seem like everything was perfectly fine.

But I wasn't going to let that be the case.

"Arrest him!" I pointed my muddy finger at Roe's face. "He's kidnapping people!"

Seeing me, Roe's body twitched. His face winced and soured. There was nothing he could do to me there. Too many witnesses.

A figure pushed from the crowd and came toward me.

The Past-Pastor, staff in hand.

"They took your daughter," I shouted, my finger still aimed at Roe's shaking head. "They drugged her and a whole bunch of them. They've all been taken away in a..."

Before I could finish a shock of fire shattered my back. I felt my whole body clamp up. My arms fell limp. My legs folded in at the knees. The ground rushed at my eyes and I collapsed in a fetal clump.

Not now, I pleaded, fighting for air. That last touch of life.

The cold started at my feet. I lost all sensation in my toes. Then in my legs. I felt I was being extruded from a casting mold. The human mold. My heart lost its rhythmic pump and I heard a sifting sound like grains of sand shaken in a paper bag.

Caspian was right when he spoke to us about the importance of how we die. Your consciousness and emotional state at the moment of death affects your transition. How prepared you are. How at peace you are. This tone travels with you and resonates into the next world. It's your death knell. And it moves to a matching tone on the other side.

In the end, it's all about the vibe.

A fog of darkness sank in. I realized I was about to die in a distressed state with so many things unresolved. I felt tormented by the truck I couldn't stop. And Tandre, Gorno, and the others, stolen away in the night. I worried for Sylvia. I didn't know what happened to the girl. Or Ray. And there was the dreadful fear that soon I'd plunge headlong into that hellish void I'd experienced when I nearly died the first time. The first bullet. The one I believed had returned for an encore.

Not this time.

Such is the fortune of being given a second death.

Although my sound was knocked out of me, two Nansa came to my rescue. The knitters untangled the knots of shock and torment that held me locked in suspension. With surgical precision they touched axis points around the crown of my head and soles of my feet. And with their touch a thousand fists inside me opened like flowers. I felt my prime tone returning and I began to sense the physical surroundings again— my body below me, dumped on the path in front of the house like a discarded overcoat.

As if given new eyes, my perception of the scene changed dramatically. It was the same place and time only a veil had been lifted. The people no longer looked like firm, flesh and bone bodies. They appeared as spheres of sonic waves with branching strands in a spectrum of lights and colors. The strands vibrated and the colors lightened and darkened in response to the sounds and sights happening around them. With this perception I could now see the true tonal architecture of human life forms.

A thick mist atomized around me and as it did, the two Nansa ushered me through the mist into a light of boundless belonging.

That's it. That's what happened. Thanks for letting me share it all with you so I could review some of my experiences. My memory is more vivid to me now than when I was, well, by your definition, alive. And so here I am in the cloud speaking to you out there on the deck of the Porch. It's funny how things play out isn't it detective?

"Yes, it certainly is, Mr. Gandy."

"Do you have questions for me?"

"I do, yes. Did you see who killed you?"

"No."

"Did you know you were shot?"

"Not at the time. Like I said, I thought the pain came from the first bullet. The one lodged next to my heart."

"And you say your back was to the south?"

"Yes. I was looking at the Past-Pastor outside the house. He was walking toward me out of the group of people from Newgrange. I know he saw me just before my body dropped to the ground."

"Anything else you can recall that might help our investigation?"

"Beyond what I've told you, no. Guess you're going to have to fill in the blanks, Detective."

"Anyone you might suspect to be your killer?"

"Suspect? Yes, but with a sliver of uncertainty. Why don't you ask Julian? Is he still around?"

"He's on our list to question."

"Then ask him. And you'd better alert police and highway patrol. Somewhere out there a large truck is traveling. The sign on the trailer says 'All Ways Moving', with a circle of arrows pointing in every direction. The truck is transporting a cargo of comatose bodies who knows where. If I were you I'd get on that right away."

"All Ways Moving."

"How's that for a contradiction."

"So, Mr. Gandy, to clarify a couple things. The last time you saw Jean Tandre alive he was...?"

"Alive? He was on his haunches, ecstatic, crawling out the tunnel from the Porch to the mudroom. But the last time I saw his body it was lying under a sheet on a rolling bed being pushed from the loading dock of the house into that truck I just described."

"And the last time you saw Sylvia?"

"She was dazed, wobbily climbing the slope around the south side of the house following a Nansa or two."

"Thank you. Thank you very much. You've been most helpful in what for me are extraordinary circumstances."

"May I ask you a couple questions, Detective?"

"By all means."

"Is the bell still here?"

"No sign of any bell, Mr. Gandy. Although we've not completed our search of the entire property."

"Any sign of the Nansa?"

"No. But you're not the first to report seeing all kinds of lights. Some folks from town swear they saw UFOs that night."

"Do you know what is being done with my body?"

"I understand it's being shipped to San Francisco. Henry Magnuson, the man you call the Past-Pastor, is handling that. He's the one who insisted we come and speak to you inside here."

"I see."

"I don't have any information about the funeral services. All I can tell you is your body is to be cremated."

"And the ashes?"

"Sorry. I don't have any more details than that."

"In a bell, please. Have my ashes sent to the Bonatti Foundry to be cast in a bell. Benni will know the one."

"I'll pass that on."

"Thank you. And what will happen to the house?"

"I can't say. Do you want to answer that, Mr. Roe?"

"Ah, Mr. Roe. I thought you might be lurking around. I could feel someone shaking in their boots while I was speaking. So, that was you protesting under your breath. Must be an unpleasant time for you."

"Most excruciating, Mr. Gandy. To hear such a flagrant distortion of things sickens me. I told you that he'd hold a grudge, Detective. Semi-trucks and comatose bodies. We cancel his project, send him on his way, and out of some deranged compulsion he concocts these grotesque lies to undermine the most extraordinary instrument ever created by man."

"I have no reason to lie, Detective. My memory is

clear. Clear as a bell."

"You are a mentally disturbed and pathological…"

"Mr. Roe, will you please just answer his question so we can move on."

"As you wish, Detective. For now we have put everything on hold. The house is closed and won't be in operation until we can locate Sylvia. We believe Jean Tandre has taken her with him."

"You don't believe this, do you Detective?"

"Evidently Mr. Tandre was seen setting fire to the silo and driving away with the girl."

"Tandre's done it before. There's a psychological term for it. It's in his profile. The upshot of it is when the time comes to part with his creations the man feels compelled to destroy them."

"Oh, spare me, Mr. Roe. Spare yourself before you get so entangled in your lies you become trapped between worlds like those comatose bodies strapped to beds in that truck. Best start now. Let your life ring true before deceit dries up your soul."

"That will be all, Mr. Gandy. Thank you again. Mr. Roe, do you want to speak to Sylvia's father?"

"I do. I call for Charles Caspian."

"Save your breath."

"Mr. Gandy, you are done. I call for Charles Caspian."

"He won't be coming. He'll only come for Sylvia. Guess you're stuck with your mother."

* * *

"Joe Gandy. I call for Joe Gandy."

"Hello?"

"Joe Gandy?"

"Someone calls me?"

"There you are. Oh, good!"

"Do I know you?"

"Yes you do. Or at least you did once. I'm Sylvia. Sylvia Caspian."

"I remember a Sylvia Caspian. She was a girl."

"That was me. Only, I'm older now."

"You certainly are. You're a young woman."

"Eighteen."

"Eighteen. What a surprise. It's good to see you."

"It's good to see you too, Joe Gandy. I've been thinking about you all these years. Can you see this? I still have your little bell."

"The crotal. Yes."

"And I often wondered if you ever reunited with your Lucia."

"You remember. How thoughtful. Yes, we did reunite. Lucia was here to greet me. It was the greatest gift I could ever ask for."

"Oh, how wonderful."

"Beyond words. We're working together here, Lucia and I. We help souls pass over whose bodies have died in traumatic circumstances."

"You must be very busy."

"We are. So, how is it that we can speak to each other? Are you on the Porch?"

"A new porch. Brand new. On another farm. A place that looks like every other farm in the country."

"But how is that? Jean Tandre is here. He's in one of the healing chambers. We've spoken. He told me what they did to him. How he drifted, detached and lost for a long time. When your father lost contact he began searching for him on this side. Jean Tandre still doesn't know where his body perished."

"I know. My father just told me."

"Of course, you've spoken with your father."

"Just now."

"He must have been happy to see you."

"Oh yes, overjoyed. He reminded me of your big bell and it all came back to me— the brilliant shower of lights that filled the Porch. Filled it with happiness."

"Do you remember striking the bell and saving my neck?"

"I remember throwing a tantrum and not being able to hear myself screaming because of the ringing in my ears."

"Well, I'm glad to see you're okay. And so now you have a new Porch."

"We do."

"What became of the other house?"

"I don't really know. Julian vanished that night. They never found the truck. It's so awful. It still haunts me. And they couldn't pin anything on Leonard. The rumor was he locked himself in the house. But that was years ago. I never went back."

"So how were you able to build this new Porch? Had Jean Tandre given you the plans?"

"Do you remember Ray? Ray Freely?"

"Ray. Yes, I remember Ray."

"Ray had the plans. He built it. And Gudrun. It was Gudrun and Ray who came for me. They gathered all the folks from Newgrange to storm the house that night. The night your body died."

"How did Ray get the plans?"

"Ray, come here."

"He's there with you?"

"Yeah-yeah-yeah, I stole the plans. So what. I would'a given 'em back to JT if he'd asked. Survival insurance, y'know."

"Hi Ray."

"Hey man. How you doin'?"

"I worried about you."

"Cut the crap. The world's goin' in the toilet and we could use one of those bells of yours. Care to tell me where I can get one?"

ACKNOWLEDGEMENTS

First and foremost, my heartfelt thanks to my wife, Veronica, for her enduring support throughout the saga of seeing the story to the end. Thanks to Patti Landres and Alta Engstrom and Ann Whelan whose thoughtful comments proved invaluable. Big thanks to Jeffrey Smith, who generously offered wise counsel and helped turn a long and rambling narrative into a readable story. Lastly, to those who fed the spirit within the story, I am deeply grateful.

www.ingramcontent.com/pod-product-compliance
Lightning Source LLC
Chambersburg PA
CBHW060545260626
47161CB00003B/1064